MIRACLE HILL

MIRACLE HILL

by

Lee Ladouceur

Copyright © 2001 by Lee Ladouceur

All rights reserved.
No part of this book may be reproduced, restored in a retrieval system, or transmitted by means, electronic, mechanical, photocopying, recording, or otherwise, without written consent from the author.

ISBN: 1-58820-324-7

1stBooks - rev. 1/16/01

ACKNOWLEDGMENTS

My Spiritual Child and friend:
    Rev. Linda Wheeler who turned me on to computers when I visited her in 1991.

My Bosses:
    The Green Thumb Agency in Kentucky who in 1994 retrained me at a time in my life when I felt my physical health was over the hill and even paid for my computer lessons. Without computer expertise this book and college could never have come to pass.
    Rosemarie Marshall, my first Literacy boss (Under Green Thumb), who gave me free reign at work to learn the computer world.
    Dean French, my second Literacy boss, (Under green Thumb) who encouraged and convinced me to go to college for a Writing Degree.

My Physician:
    Dr. Maxwell Brown of Bardstown who has gotten me back on my feet, running on full steam again, and encouraged me to go on to college.

My Proof readers:
    Sam Rosenberg who generously gave me my first computer, keeps me supplied with paper, ink ribbons, tuna fish, and spurs me on every time I get literary lazy.
    Rev. Ray Dymun my best literary critic.
    Peggy Walker my dearest librarian friend.
    Betty Florence who is a retired Missionary, School Teacher, and Homeschooler and my E-mail-inspirational buddy.

The following have listened to my stories as I wrote them and kept me true to the happenings.

My daughters <u>Lois Dymun, Gwen Cooper, and Beth Beaulieu</u>.

My sons who encourage me to publish my stories.
<u>Edward and William Harrison</u>.

My grandson <u>Charles Edward Harrison</u> who as a nine yr. old sat with rapt attention and complete adoration of God and me as he heard me teach the stories in my Texas Bible classes. He was the first one to encourage me to write them down.

<u>And to all the others</u> who encouraged me in any way to remember, write, and publish what the Lord has done for me.

Dedicated

to
my
children
Mary Gale, Charles Clarence, George Robert, Michael Allen,
William Paul, Mary Beth, Mary Lois, Mary Gwen, Edward
Wayne.

and
all of Edward's
children

plus
all
my
many
Spiritual
children

Psalms 127:3 Lo, children [are] an heritage of the LORD: [and] the fruit of the womb [is his] reward.

Psalms 127:4 As arrows [are] in the hand of a mighty man; so [are] children of the youth

Psalms 127:5 Happy [is] the man that hath his quiver full of them: they shall not be ashamed, but they shall speak with the enemies in the gate.

CONTENTS

ACKNOWLEDGMENTS v
DEDICATION vii
FORWARD xiii

Chapter 1
    ANGELS 1

Chapter 2
    TOYS 3

Chapter 3
    CIGARETTES 5

Chapter 4
    BISCUITS 9

Chapter 5
    HIP REPLACEMENT 13

Chapter 6
    BILLS 17

Chapter 7
    BIOPSY 21

Chapter 8
    TELEVISION 25

Chapter 9
    MUSCLES HEALED 29

Chapter 10
    SOCIAL SECURITY 35

Chapter 11
 ATTITUDE CHANGE 39

Chapter 12
 THE BAR 43

Chapter 13
 THE JAR 47

Chapter 14
 TITHE 51

Chapter 15
 $500.00 53

Chapter 16
 DEER SEASON 57

Chapter 17
 TEACH 61

Chapter 18
 FIRE 65

Chapter 19
 TEMPER 69

Chapter 20
 CLOTHES 73

Chapter 21
 $50.00 77

Chapter 22
 CHICKEN 81

Chapter 23
  RAINBOW 85

Chapter 24
  TRACTOR 87

Chapter 25
  STRAWBERRIES 91

Chapter 26
  SLOW DOWN 95

Chapter 27
  COWS 99

Chapter 28
  WINDOW 103

Chapter 29
  HEART ATTACK 105

Chapter 30
  INSULIN 109

Chapter 31
  WOODS 113

Chapter 32
  TRIP 117

Chapter 33
  SAWDUST 119

EPILOGUE 123

FORWARD

Edward died four years after we were married. That was 16 years ago and I still carry a love for him that is so satisfying that I have stayed a widow all these years. He and I grew-up together in the ways of the Lord. It was he that dubbed our home-place "Miracle Hill" due to all the wonderful ways God answered our prayers.

Ours is a story of the love of God drawing two sinners into the Kingdom of God and the process He used to change us...miracles. It would be impossible not to love someone who does great feats for you in the face of insurmountable odds...God did this for Edward and I.

Edward and I had left our respective walks of life carrying the excess baggage of pain, distrust, and unhappiness over our loses. He came from a big, tough city of the North while I had grown up in a quiet, sparsely populated town of the South. We were basically very different but we met because God decreed it.

In one of God's visits to me, He told me to teach sanctification. He said, "The husband sanctifies the wife and the wife sanctifies the husband. Little did I know that to teach it, I would first have to live it. Proverbs 27:17 says, "Iron sharpeneth iron; so a man sharpeneth the countenance of his friend." Edward and I both had iron wills, and God used them to sharpen each of us. I cried buckets of tears, threatened to leave more times than I care to admit, and was thoroughly upset because the only choice in life that held any promise of happiness was to go on with God ...and Edward.

I have tried to write about our pain of change in the exact expressions that were used at the time in hopes of endearing the stories to your memory. Here and there I have had to shorten some of the stories to keep the pace fast for the reader but other than this everything happened just as I have written them.

If the Lord permits, there will be more books to follow this one since it would be impossible to put all that God has done for me in one book.

It is my earnest hope that by revealing my sins and sick attitudes that you, my readers, can learn from my mistakes and thus make your journey in sanctification easier.

Chapter 1
ANGELS

Hebrews 1:13 But to which of the angels said he at any time, Sit on my right hand, until I make thine enemies thy footstool?

Hebrews 1:14 Are they not all ministering spirits, sent forth to minister for them who shall be heirs of salvation?

Luke 4:10 For it is written, He shall give his angels charge over thee, to keep thee:

Mark 1:13 And he was there in the wilderness forty days, tempted of Satan; and was with the wild beasts; and the angels ministered unto him.

When I married Edward he was on disability due to a heart valve replacement and diabetes. We used his monthly check to cover the house expenses, gas for the car and medicine. This left us about five dollars for entertainment. Our big treat once a month was to ride to Gaylord, Michigan, which was thirty miles away and buy a donut and a cup of coffee for each of us. We liked to do this about two in the morning when everything was quiet and we could look at the deer along the roads.

One winter night, as we drove to the donut shop, we began to improvise verses to the song, "God Is So Good." By the time we had reached Gaylord we were really charged-up in the Lord.

As we sat and talked to the other night-owls like us, and witnessed about Jesus in our lives, the time slipped by without our realizing it...we had been there over three hours. A man came into the shop stomping snow, with the wind nearly ripping off the door. We were all shocked to see that a blizzard had settled in while we had basked in the warmth of friendship and coffee.

Saying our good-byes, we jumped into our truck and headed for home. The snow was half way up the tires, the wind was biting cold and the visibility almost zero. To keep from being scared we began to sing our songs again.

Three quarters of the way home we had to climb a steep hill that had no guard rails, no sand sitting by, and no way to get a running start. We were half way up this hill when Edward stopped singing and said, "Dear, you better start praying. We have no power and this truck is sliding sideways and backwards. We are going to go over that cliff if God doesn't do something."

"Oh Edward, that is easy for the angels to take care of," I said. "Angels, give us a push, in the name of Jesus." The truck lurched forward and began to pick up speed.

Right before we topped the hill Edward shouted, "Dear, you better tell them to slow down or we will whip all over the road at the top"....I did and they did.

Close to home Edward said, "Dear, don't forget to have the angels get us up our hill." Well, frankly, I didn't care whether they did or didn't since we were within walking distance of the house. We got half way up our driveway and the truck motor died, never to start again that night.

The next morning Edward went out to work on the truck so he could use its snow plow to clear our drive way. About thirty minutes later he was back inside with his eyes as big as silver dollars. He had something in his hand.

He said, "Dear, it really WAS the angels that pushed us home. This is the noise I heard half way up that first hill." He held out his hand and there was the truck's distributor cap busted in three pieces. He said, "That truck should never have gotten us home."

God is faithful.

Chapter 2
TOYS

2 Corinthians 12:1 It is not expedient for me doubtless to glory. I will come to visions and revelations of the Lord.

Hosea 12:10 I have also spoken by the prophets, and I have multiplied visions, and used similitudes, by the ministry of the prophets.

Joel 2:28 And it shall come to pass afterward, [that] I will pour out my spirit upon all flesh; and your sons and your daughters shall prophesy, your old men shall dream dreams, your young men shall see visions:

Edward had been repairing an old car body, getting it ready to paint. He came into the house asking if we had an old wire brush anywhere. As I said, "No," a strange mental picture of a wire brush appeared in my mind. It was almost as if I could reach out and touch it.

About an hour later, he came back inside, looking for an extension cord. "No", I said, "and in fact, I need one myself." Once more I received a strange mental picture in my mind. Only this time I saw two extension cords, so vivid that like before, I could almost touch them.

It was the middle of the month and our entertainment allowance had been spent already. I had been studying the Bible about eight hours a day for a couple of weeks and I needed some time out. Edward had managed to pick up an odd job, and knowing my time-out need, he offered to treat me to a donut and coffee in Gaylord.

So, on the evening of the wire brush and extension cord dilemma, we drove the thirty miles to Gaylord, to visit our favorite donut shop. It was close to 12 midnight when we left, and after staying a couple of hours at the donut shop, we started home. As always, we were singing every Christian song we could think of.

As we cruised along we passed some large bags of garbage piled up on the roadside all by themselves. There were no houses in sight nor driveways...only open fields for miles around. On top of the pile were big, dented Tonka Trucks for children. As we zoomed past, Edward said, "Dear, did you see that?" "I sure did." I answered. He said," You want to go back and get them? I can bump them out and they will be just like new." To which I replied, "I'm game if you are. Never let it be said that I'm a "wet-blanket."

There were four of us couples from the church we were attending who had started meeting in our homes for Bible classes.

Two of the couples brought their children and Edward and I had no toys for them to play with when they met at our house. The toys on top of the sacks looked like the perfect solution.

As we were loading up, Edward came upon a small box that had pop-toys for small babies in it. He wanted to know if we should take them considering that there were no children that little in our group. I said, "Sure, Love, we will give them to somebody."

The next morning Edward went downstairs to check out his garbage-goodies. In moments he was back, with his silver-dollar eye balls again.

He said, "Dear, you will never guess what was under those pop-toys." He tilted the box over toward me...snuggled in the bottom of the box were one wire brush and two extension cords.

God had been busy in our behalf.

Chapter 3
CIGARETTES

Ephesians 4:30 And grieve not the holy Spirit of God, whereby ye are sealed unto the day of redemption.

Galatians 5:16 [This] I say then, Walk in the Spirit, and ye shall not fulfil the lust of the flesh.

1 Corinthians 6:19 What? know ye not that your body is the temple of the Holy Ghost [which is] in you, which ye have of God, and ye are not your own?

All my remembering-years I saw my Father smoke cigarettes. My favorite aunt smoked. It seemed to make her look so cool. When I grew up almost all of my friends smoked. Let's face it..it was the in-thing of fashion at that point in the world's timetable.

When I got my first job at an Ice Cream Plant, everyone who smoked was permitted to take twice as many breaks as those of us who did not smoke. I spoke to my boss often about the unfairness of this. I got nowhere.

So finally, I said, "Tomorrow I will be a smoker." My boss just scoffed at this.

The next day I marched out with the rest of the crowd and lit up my Camel. To my boss's dismay, for the rest of my tenure there I went on smoke-breaks just like the rest of the workers did. I felt like I had righted justice single-handily.

Little did I know that it would be impossible to lay them down once I quit work. Nor did I realize that the five breaks-of-cigarettes would grow to two and one half packs a day.

My lungs tried to tell me to stop smoking. I just took more antibiotics. Asthma and bronchitis did their best to convince me to quit. I doubled up on the cough medicine. Doctors tried to scare me with threats like cancer. I was immovable.

When I met Edward he smoked as much as I did. In July of '79, between puffs and coughs we were married....by a preacher who smoked.

One summer day, Edward made the statement, "When cigarettes go up to one dollar a pack we are going to stop smoking." This sounded fair so I agreed to it.

The next Spring cigarettes went up to one dollar a pack. Edward came home from the grocery and announced, "You are going to stop smoking."

I said, "What about you?" "No", he said.

I could feel the old tapes replaying once again. I was back in the Ice Cream factory. And here was my unfair "boss" once more.

Annoyance tickled my nervous system. I felt my eye lids squint up to little slits. I was getting set for battle.

"And, just WHY should I quit and you not?" I asked through clenched teeth.

"Because I pay for them, that is why." he smirked at me. Plainly, it was time to take this matter to a higher court. I turned around and headed to the conference room...my bedroom. Sitting on my bed, I looked up and whispered, "Father God, did You hear what that son of yours just said?" And I poured out the whole sordid story to God just as if He didn't already know.

God is very fair. He heard me out. When I was through complaining I said, "Ok, God what am I supposed to do now?"

He spoke to my spirit and said, "Quit." I couldn't believe my ears. I countered, "But God, this is not fair." That is as far as I got.

"It is Me who wants you to quit smoking. I just went through Edward to get your attention," God's sweet voice said.

"Well, God, why didn't You just say so. I would have quit if I had known it was You that wanted me to," I whined...

"I did say so. I told you in My Word; that you are the temple of the Holy Spirit, and not to defile it."

"Oh, yes," I said. He went on, "I also sent you doctors, magazine articles, newspaper stories and testimonies from former smokers. You chose to ignore all of them."

God was right and I knew it, but I just wasn't ready to concede yet. "Then if it is You that wants me to quit smoking why didn't You have Edward tell me to quit in a sweet tone of voice like Yours? He was so ugly about it."

To which God replied, "You wouldn't have listened." When I heard this I knew I was defeated. I finally got a better attitude and then threw away my cigarettes. This act blessed me with healthier lungs, no more bronchitis, and a closer walk with Jesus...and later, God dealt with Edward and HIS cigarettes.

Chapter 4
BISCUITS

Acts 22:14 And he said, The God of our fathers hath chosen thee, that thou shouldest know his will, and see that Just One, and shouldest hear the voice of his mouth.

Hebrews 3:15 While it is said, To day if ye will hear his voice, harden not your hearts, as in the provocation.

Deuteronomy 26:17 Thou hast avouched the LORD this day to be thy God, and to walk in his ways, and to keep his statutes, and his commandments, and his judgments, and to hearken unto his voice:

Being on a limited income is better than having no income, but it does have its downside. When the price of anything goes up, the amount of spending-cash stays the same.

There had been an increase in the price of groceries. The amount we had budgeted for them just wasn't enough to last the month out. So the time came when we ran out of breakfast food.

I had watched my mother during the War years as she improvised great meals out of what seemed to be an empty cabinet. She had managed to pass this ability on to me.

In lieu of easy-to-fix breakfast cereal, and with great pains, I whipped up home-made biscuits, and white milk gravy. I peeled fresh apples and made them into a biscuit spread with whipped butter that I had created myself. It was quite a treat and lots of work. The first morning Edward ate everything with much oooooh'ing and ahhhhh'ing.

On the second morning he sat down in front of our picture window, and surveying the countryside below said, "Boy, I sure am lucky to have such a wonderful wife. I'll bet every farmer around here had to get up this morning and fix himself cold cereal for breakfast, while I laid in bed and my wife fixed ME hot biscuits and gravy."

Of course I beamed with pleasure that Edward had finally stopped criticizing everything ...only it didn't last.

The third morning he said, "I only want one biscuit, and the gravy is too thick."

"Feed one of the biscuits to the dog," I said.

Giving me his I'm-out-to-get-you look, he said, "I don't want to give my biscuit to the dog."

I said, "Edward, I can only cut the recipe down so far, two biscuits being the smallest amount I can work with." I could tell Edward was not happy with this answer.

That night I read a book on "Praise. "It had insisted that we give praise to God in all things, good and bad. If we would do this, God would come on the scene and change things. In the peacefulness of the moment I had agreed to give this a try.

Breakfast time came again. Instead of cutting out two small biscuits, I rolled and patted the dough into one nice big round biscuit.

Our two hens had finally managed to lay an egg between them. Edward could have eggs twice a week, so I served the biscuit with a nice fried egg, fixed just the way he liked.

"The biscuit is too tough, and the gravy is too thick," he mouthed. Immediately my eye lids became slits and my teeth clenched in anger. In my mind I said, "Lord, there he goes again. This is not fair. What am I going to do with him?" I heard the words, "Praise Me."

"You have got to be kidding me, Lord. Praise you for Edward? Come now." Again I heard, "Praise Me."

"Ok, Lord, I did agree last night." So, through clenched teeth, I hissed out, "Praise the Lord for you, Edward." As soon as I spoke, all the anger and hurt feelings left me. I said, "Wow Lord, it works. You have changed Edward. Thank you."

The following morning we went through the same thing again. "The biscuit is too large and the gravy is too thin."

Once more I appealed to God in my thought life. "Father God, I thought You changed Edward. He is still complaining." Again I heard the words, "Praise Me." To which I put up the same argument as the day before.

Finally giving in, and again through clenched teeth I said, "Praise the Lord for you Edward." Once more the bad feeling immediately left me and I felt fine. I KNEW this time that God had changed Edward.

Breakfast time came around again. This time, ".. the biscuit is too crumbly and the apples are too dry." I was furious. I said, "God, this man doesn't deserve to have someone fix him ANY food...and I thought You changed him. What am I going to do now? No! Don't tell me. I know. You want me to praise You again."

This time I unclenched my teeth, managed a sick smile, and said, "Praise the Lord! I see I still have my complaining husband." And like the times before I instantly felt fine and full of joy.

We always finished breakfast by saying our morning prayers together before we left the table. At the end of Edward's prayer on this particular morning he said, "And thank you God, for giving me my wonderful wife, who puts up with me so well. She is always full of smiles and cheerfulness. She cheers me up." Edward hadn't even been aware of the inward struggle that had been going on between God and me."

When cornered into a situation that wasn't to Edward's liking, he still continued to complain. But I had learned a new way to handle the stress during these times so that I could hold on to the joy that made and continues to make my life with Jesus so enjoyable. God taught me that He may not change others, but He will always change me ...if I am willing.

Chapter 5
HIP REPLACEMENT

Psalms 22:3 But thou [art] holy, [O thou] that inhabitest the praises of Israel.

Psalms 50:23 Whoso offereth praise glorifieth me: and to him that ordereth [his] conversation [aright] will I shew the salvation of God.

Hebrews 13:15 By him therefore let us offer the sacrifice of praise to God continually, that is, the fruit of [our] lips giving thanks to his name.

"You will have to have a total hip replacement," the doctor stated to Edward, "and it will have to be done by a surgeon in a hospital down-state from here." We went home and began making preparations to close up our house for a few weeks.

We farmed-out our rooster and two hens and left enough bird seed on our porch to feed half the geese in Canada. We were putting a four-by-eight sheet of ply-wood over the sliding glass door in the downstairs to deter homesteaders...when it happened. The end of the board I was carrying slipped and it came crashing down on the arch of my foot.

Dropping the board, I grabbed up my hurt foot and started dancing around on the good one groaning out, "Praise the Lord. unnnnh.. Praise the Lord. ugggggh...ahhhhgh.. PRAISE THE LORD... ohhhhh...Praise the Lord!"

Through all this pain and agony, I began to hear laughter getting louder and louder. When my eyes could finally focus through the pain and tears, I saw Edward doubled over and holding his sides while he had a laughing-fit.

"What is so funny?", I snarled. I shouldn't have asked.

He said, "You are." Then he proceeded to give me an "Edward" demonstration of how silly I looked, hopping on one foot, with his face all screwed up in agony, and praising God all at the same time. I got mad.

"Well, the Bible said Praise God in ALL things, and that means the bad as well as the good...and that is what I'm going to do, whether you find it ridiculous or not," I hissed out at him.

As I stomped off in a huff, my foot momentarily hurt and then it was ok. I actually forgot about it as we took our baths, headed to our destination, and fell in bed as soon as we arrived.

We had to be at the hospital very early the next morning so we sponged bathed and took off. When I got home that night it was late and I was so exhausted that I just went to bed, dispensing with a bath.

We were staying in a private home that a church had supplied for us. The lady was old and liked everything very quiet. She had an old time bath tub that took forever to fill up. Since I came in very late at night and I had to be at the hospital before daylight, I just washed a few places and dressed. I did not remove my socks.

Let me stop here and explain about a very peculiar part of my body...my feet. My feet turn to ice when the first leaf begins to change color in the Fall. They only get warm when the robins have their first set of babies in the Spring, or when my socks get 3 days old.

I grew up in Louisville, Kentucky in a time era that a lot of people still dragged out the old wash tub on Saturday nights and took a good blood-warm bath. My father was prosperous enough to afford a bath tub where we could bath every day or twice if we were so mind to...but I was not. For me to remove the socks from my ice cold feet was pure pain.

They never smelled bad, because my feet never sweated, even in the hot summertime. So, no matter how hot the water was, or how warm the bath room was, my feet were like chunks of ice in winter. Now, if they were this cold in Kentucky, you can just imagine how frozen they were in upper Michigan. Which brings us back to Edward's operation.

It was three days before Edward was stabilized and I finely had time in the morning to draw a tub full of nice warm bath water. As I removed my socks for the quick plunge, I was shocked. The foot that I had dropped the board on three and a half days before was a bruised mess. It had turned shades of deep red, blue, purple, yellow, greenish, and black.

I had been a medicine-aide for four years. I had seen better feet than this packed in ice, and held up in a sling...with much pain medicine on the side. My foot had not hurt one bit from the time I took the second step. ..nor had it swelled. I actually had not known anything was wrong with it, other than the initial pain. God had seen me through, just because I had praised Him even in the bad times. My heart swelled with love for God.

Tears of gratitude slowly ran down my face. He and I had a worship service right there in a warm bath tub and my birthday suit, with only the angels looking on.

I now understood what He meant when He told the Samaritan woman in John 4:21-24 that it is not WHERE we worship God, but HOW we worship Him...in spirit and truth.

God the healer had been on the scene.

Chapter 6
BILLS

Psalms 4:3 But know that the LORD hath set apart him that is godly for himself: the LORD will hear when I call unto him.

2 Corinthians 4:17 For our light affliction, which is but for a moment, worketh for us a far more exceeding [and] eternal weight of glory;

2 Corinthians 4:18 While we look not at the things which are seen, but at the things which are not seen: for the things which are seen [are] temporal; but the things which are not seen [are] eternal.

My husband and I had many medical expenses. He took heart medicine and insulin shots every day. And even though he was on disability, he had to pay for all of his medicine. I also took medication every day and had to pay for my medicine. When looking at it from a prescription standpoint, we were a pharmacist's delight.

When we first married, we kept up with our drug bills. But as time went on, we began to drop behind. So, to cut down on some of our expenses we bought a wood burning stove and began to use the timber on our land to heat with, instead of the expensive oil. But then our car quit. We had to buy parts for it. It seemed as if each month brought with it new money problems. Our druggist was kind enough to "ok" credit for us.

The day finally came that our drug bill reached three hundred dollars. I really felt bad about it. We had gone from charging just medicine to charging things that we would have normally bought at the grocery store if there had been enough money. Now, we were way in over our heads. Even though we paid some on it each month, the bill just kept climbing.

During this time, we were learning about the Grace of God. The Bible was teaching us that God loves us right where we are, even with all our sins. And after we accept His Son as our

Savior, He will change us...gradually. But the amazing thing about this is God never gets angry at us nor condemns us during this process.

Well now, this all seemed too good to be true. Most of the people I had ever had any dealings with would get a little nasty with me if I didn't live up to their standards, especially people I had made a promise to.

Now, along comes God and tells me He is not like this. No way could I believe this...I turned into a Biblical doubting-Thomas overnight.

Finally I said, "Ok Lord, show me this is true. Just show me one person like this. Edward and I are not like this and the people in our church aren't either." God did show me one.

The one turned out to be our druggist. In all that time of charging, Brother Bob never once reminded us of how much we owed him...nor did he complain about the unnecessary things we began charging. His attitude toward us stayed the same. He treated us with respect.

The Bible tells us that God wants to come and dwell inside us. Now, if this is true, then people should be able to see something different about a Christian...don't you agree? Well, I saw something different in our druggist.

Like I said earlier, we were now facing a three hundred dollar charge account at the drug store. I dreaded to even give the druggist our small, pitiful payment.

On one of our monthly trips to pay on this bill, I walked up to the counter and started to hand the clerk my payment. The druggist came forward and said, "Don't take her money. She doesn't owe anything." I looked at him hard to see if he had developed a mental problem that had gone undetected until now. He looked the same.

Knowing what a joker he always was, I said, "Ok, Brother, quit the joking. Just take my payment".

He said, "I'm serious. Someone came in here and paid your bill." With that, he turned his ledger book around. The page was opened to our account and scribbled across the bottom of the page was...Paid in full by Jesus.

This happened several times more before we moved away from East Jordan, Michigan.

Now, you are probably saying, "Oh well, the druggist was your friend, and he paid it. That is no miracle." That could be true. But, I came from a background where we had a doctor, druggist and lawyer for friends and when hard times hit for me, I still had to pay what I owed them. These also, were church-going people.

I prefer to believe that in answer to my prayer, I had been exposed to the "Grace of God," in a white coat behind a medicine counter.

Chapter 7
BIOPSY

Mark 4:40 And he said unto them, Why are ye so fearful? how is it that ye have no faith?

Habakkuk 2:4 Behold, his soul [which] is lifted up is not upright in him: but the just shall live by his faith.

Mark 11:22 And Jesus answering saith unto them, Have faith in God.

In 1969 I began to have mild pain in all my muscles and through the years it had steadily gotten worse. By the time 1979 came around the doctors had me on Cortisone once a day, prescription pain killers four times a day and Tylenol in between. All this medicine took the edge off the pain, but nothing removed it entirely. At times, my muscles were so painful I had to go to bed and take antibiotics to fight the inflammation.

Finally, after ten years, a doctor came up with a diagnosis, but it would take a muscle biopsy to confirm it. I had no insurance to pay for the biopsy so I was advised to apply for medical aide. The agency I applied to told me that I would have to be disabled to get Medical-aid and to be classified as disabled, I would have to have a muscle biopsy done. Clearly, the biopsy would have to be put on hold, while everyone tries to decide which comes first...the chicken and then the egg...or is it the egg and then the chicken....?

My husband and I were now heavy into the Bible and teaching tapes. We also looked forward to visiting each week with a small group of Believers who had formed and stayed on the phone to one another the rest of the week. We were bursting at the seams with praise reports of miracles among us. Our faith was really growing.

Christmas was a week away and once again, I was flat in bed. Edward said, "Dear, you must get that biopsy and see if something can be done for you."

To which I replied, "Ok Edward, I'll make the appointment tomorrow and we will depend on God to see us through for financing."

Two days later, I walked into a surgeon's office and after listening to my symptoms, he agreed that I needed a biopsy. He then proceeded to fill out the papers for tests to be run and to be admitted to the hospital. He said, "What is the name of your insurance company?" At this point I said, "We don't have insurance of any kind. But I'll tell you what we do have...plenty of faith in God. If you are willing to wait for your money, God will pay my bill."

The surgeon was Jewish and everyone knows that surgeons rarely smile as a general rule, even Jewish ones. The corners of this doctor's mouth twitched, as if to smile, as he twirled his pen in his hand. He sat quietly, not looking up and finally said, "How soon do you want to be admitted?" As we made plans for the next day, I asked him how long I would be in there and he said, "You will be there five days."

Well, I had seven surgeries of different sorts, and nine children, so a biopsy was practically nothing to me. Raising my eyebrows, I said, "Whoa, now. Just because God is paying the bill doesn't mean that we have to get carried away here. Can't we economize a little?" At this point, the corners of his mouth quivered greatly.

After a long silence with more twirling of his pen, he said, "Ok, we will do this on an out-patient basis. You go to the hospital tomorrow at nine a. m. and you will be back out about eleven a.m., and I will cut my fee in half."

To which I replied, "That's much better." I didn't tell him, but I never even THOUGHT about the reduction of his bill. It was only the hospital bill that had me concerned.

Then he dropped the bomb shell. He said, "When you get home you will have to stay in bed for five days. Someone will have to help you up and down when you go to the bathroom, but you can't stay up any longer than that."

Now I was suspicious. I said, "Is this major surgery, by any chance?"

"Yes it is," he said. "I will cut the main muscle in your shoulder and neck area."

"Will I have any morphine of any kind to take home with me? My neighbor is a nurse and she can give me the shots."

"No. You will only have the pain killers that you already are taking and you can't increase them."

I gulped and broke out in a cold sweat. Inwardly I was screaming, "God, what are you doing to me?" I watched that Jew sitting there, just waiting to see what I would say. He was putting my boast-of-faith to the test. He wasn't about to give an inch more. I even suspected that he too, was talking to God....

I did the only thing I could...I appealed to MY Jew. I said, "Jesus, don't you fail me now." Finally, after what SEEMED like an hour of a stand-off, I agreed to the doctor's terms.

When I awakened from surgery the next morning I felt fine. As I raised up from the stretcher to go home, nausea hit me full force. I lay back down and said, "Woah, Holy Spirit, this was not part of the deal. You have to help me to get home without getting sick and with no pain. You are my only hope." I reminded Him of a few healing scripture promises and we headed for home without throwing up and with no pain.

For the next week I had absolutely no pain anywhere. The only way I could tell anything was different was by the heaviness in my arm and shoulder. The Holy Spirit of God was on the job making God's Word come to pass in my body.

While I was recuperating after the surgery, I received a phone call from the medical-aid processors. They had reviewed my case and had decided they would give me medical coverage, even without the biopsy that was needed. AND they would date it back to when I had first applied for it, close to a year before. Almost as an after thought they said, "Oh, yes, we have approved your husband's card also."

As I hung up the phone, I did my usual thing when confronted with a genuine miracle of God's. I screamed...then I called the doctor to tell him that God had indeed paid his bill.

I am in love with the most wonderful Jew in the whole world...Jesus, the Faithful.

Chapter 8
TELEVISION

Joshua 24:15 And if it seem evil unto you to serve the LORD, choose you this day whom ye will serve; whether the gods which your fathers served that [were] on the other side of the flood, or the gods of the Amorites, in whose land ye dwell: but as for me and my house, we will serve the LORD.

Proverbs 4:26 Ponder the path of thy feet, and let all thy ways be established.

Proverbs 4:27 Turn not to the right hand nor to the left: remove thy foot from evil.

It was Friday and Edward had been watching television for over two hours while I was trying to study and pray. My bedroom was in the back of the house and even with the door closed and music playing in my ear, I could still hear the noise of the TV...I got mad.

But, let me give you some background as to why I was upset. Months before, God had dealt with me about watching television. He had pointed out to me that I was filling my mind with life styles that were against His Spiritual principles, so I began to censor what I watched. I would go to my room and read my Bible instead of watching whatever my husband happened to turn on.

Before long Edward started complaining about my absence. I explained to him what God had said and I agreed to a compromise. "If you can find anything decent on the television, I will be more than happy to join you."

Edward began to do better. He changed from smut to Grisly Adams and game shows...but the commercials were just retched. I was told I would have a horrible day unless I showered with a certain soap and if I wasn't as sexy as the long, skinny blond spread all over the car I could NEVER sell anything. I would also loose my joy and pout if I didn't have a Big Mac from

25

McDonalds...right then. We won't even discuss the breakfast cereal commercials.

Back to my room I went and, as before, Edward began to grumble. So I compromised again...I would run to my room when the commercials came on and he would yell for me when they went off. The time came when I stopped compromising and chose the Bible over Edward and the TV At this point all hell broke loose.

As I read my Bible the noise of the TV would get louder. I would ask Edward to turn it down and he would tell me he had not touched it. I tried putting cotton in my ears and this helped for a few days. Then the sound increased again...and this brings us up to the Friday that I finally got angry.

I sat down on the side of my bed and began to remind God of His Word. I was looking upward and speaking out-loud in a very angry whisper. I said, "God, You said in Your Word that Edward and I are the same flesh. That the two are made one when they marry. If that is true then Edward should not be watching TV either. He is the other half of me. Now God, You are not a man that can lie, You said. So, I want You to back up Your Word. Make Edward stop watching television also. You are a God of fairness and justice and it is not fair that I quit and Edward not. So, please do something about this right away. I know. Blow up the TV...only don't let Edward get hurt. Thank you God."

After that conversation I went on to bed fully expecting God to get rid of that bone-of-contention. The next morning was Saturday and we came out of our respective rooms to have breakfast. As we passed the television Edward stopped and turned it on. He NEVER watched TV on Saturdays. I became so upset that I turned around and went back to my bedroom for a conference with God.

Through clenched teeth and flared nostrils, I reminded God of our agreement the night before and informed Him that something had backfired. Edward was now watching more television than usual. Again I demanded justice and asked Him to blow that thing up quickly...but to not hurt Edward.

Once more I headed to the kitchen. Just as I went behind Edward's chair the picture on the television screen shrank into a small circle and then disappeared. Edward yelled, "Look Dear, the television stopped. I wonder what's wrong." I wanted to laugh out loud, but the Holy Spirit checked me.

Instead I said, "Maybe God doesn't want you to watch TV Sweetheart." Edward said nothing as he went over to the door switch that controlled that particular floor plug and began to take the cover off. A shocked look came on his face and he said, "Look Dear, the wire is not on. That plug could never have worked."

To which I replied, "Did you ever stop and think that maybe God doesn't want you to watch TV Love?"

Very crossly he said, "Yea, yea," as he headed down the stairs to turn off the electric. As soon as he had the plug working again, he promptly turned the television back on and sat down to watch it.

Well, I was really upset now. Back to the conference room I went to tell God about this latest event. Once more I reminded The Almighty of His Word, His promises, His faithfulness and His truthfulness. Then I explained to Him the fact that if His Word was true like He says it is, then He had to back it up and that was all there was to it. I knew my rights and I was not asking anything against His will, nor his Word. I left that room fortified with courage, confidence, and joy that my God would do wonders for me.

As I walked behind Edward's chair again, the TV picture disappeared into a little circle of nothingness just as before. To which he said, "Dear, look at the TV. The picture is gone again." I wanted to laugh out loud so badly I almost choked, but again the Spirit checked me.

I said, "Are you going to take the door switch cover off again, Love?" To which Edward said in a loud, scared voice, "No!" Instead he got up, searched for an extension cord and then plugged the TV into a different circuit. Smiling, he sat down to watch it.

I was dumb-founded...I couldn't believe what I was seeing. The fight went out of me and hurt and disappointment set in. I went to the kitchen and fixed Edward's breakfast. When he sat down to eat he said, "Aren't you going to eat, Dear?"

I could barely answer, "No, Love, I'm not hungry. I don't feel well. I'm going back to bed."

My broken heart and I crawled into the bed, and pulling up the covers I just let the tears roll down on both sides of my face. As I looked up God's way, I whimpered to Him, "I can't believe You didn't do Your part. I am crushed. Your Word is not true. You ARE a man that can lie. I don't ever want to get up again." All this time tears were pouring out of my eyes from deep inside me. I wasn't crying or sobbing on the emotional side of me.

This was from my spirit.

After Edward finished his breakfast and checked on me, he headed to town like he always did on Saturdays. A bunch of his old cronies always got together at a certain restaurant and relived their deer hunting experiences all over again. This went on for at least 3 hours. It took only 15 minutes to get from our house to this restaurant.

This Saturday, in the space of forty minutes Edward came charging through our front door hollering, "Dear, there is a man up at the restaurant that wants to trade a deer rifle for a television. Do you mind if we trade him ours?"

After he and the television were out of earshot, I jumped out of that bed screaming, shouting praises, and running through our house like a child does on the first day of deep snow-fall. This is better known in the Christian circles as a "Hallelujah Party".

God had shown Himself strong in my behalf again.

Chapter 9
MUSCLES HEALED

Isaiah 53:5 But he [was] wounded for our transgressions, [he was] bruised for our iniquities: the chastisement of our peace [was] upon him; and with his stripes we are healed.

Mark 6:13 And they cast out many devils, and anointed with oil many that were sick, and healed [them].

1 Peter 2:24 Who his own self bare our sins in his own body on the tree, that we, being dead to sins, should live unto righteousness: by whose stripes ye were healed.

After the muscle biopsy around Christmas of '79 the doctors finally decided I had a degenerative muscle disease. One is born with it but it doesn't show up until one is in their late 30's...the same years that mine had reared its ugly head. I was given an assortment of medication that only dulled the pain...it never went away entirely.

From the time I received the Holy Spirit into my life in the Fall of 1979, I began to study everything I could find about "Divine Healing." In the Spring of 1980, I was given a book about healing by a Presbyterian Minister in Canton, Ohio. I put it in my read-it-later stack.

It was now October, the same year, and I was in bed again taking another round of antibiotics. Having exhausted all the other reading material on healing, I began to read the book I had gotten in Ohio. I had only read three or four pages when the verse from Hebrews 13:8, "Jesus Christ the same yesterday, and today, and for ever," caught my attention.

I laid the book down and said, "Yes, Father God, this is true...and that means You still heal today. Well, You are either going to heal me or I'm going to die, but I am NOT going back to the doctor and I am NOT going to take any more antibiotics." I folded my arms across my chest, and clamped my jaw shut since there was nothing more to discuss...it was settled as far as I was concerned.

The next morning I got up to take my pain medication and just as I raised the pill to my mouth, the sweetest male voice I had ever heard said, "Don't take that."

The doctors had tried for years to get me to stop my prescription pain medication for a period of time, so I wouldn't become immune to it, but that had been impossible. This voice was so compelling and loving that I had no problem complying with His wishes.

I fixed breakfast and just as I raised the fork to my mouth, the same sweet voice said, "Don't eat." I had been raised in a religion that insisted that we fast for certain things and times. I suffered greatly with stomach pains through those times and as often as not, would have to abandon the fast. This time I had no problem whatsoever.

As I lay back down in bed, the inside of my body suddenly caught on fire from head to toe. I screamed for my husband, "Edward! Come quick and bring the thermometer. I think I'm dying. There is a terrible fever inside me." When he took my temperature, it was normal.

All of a sudden I knew what it was. I said, "Either the Holy Spirit is healing me or I am dying and I don't really care which. It is so wonderful." I felt like I was on a high like one gets from either drugs or alcohol. The pain was all gone...and I had the giggles.

Every hour I would feel compelled to get up and drink a ten ounce glass of water. I had a terrible experience with drinking water when I was a child and since that time I NEVER drank plain water...I would gag on it. But as I drank the water out of our well, it tasted different than usual...so wonderfully SWEET that I actually thirsted for it.

Each time, just as I touched my lips with the glass, I would hear that same SWEET VOICE saying, "This is LIVING WATER." This went on for three days and part of each night. I experienced no drug-withdrawal symptoms, hunger or stomach pains from fasting.

On the third day at 5:00 p.m. I was lying in the bed just talking to God, "Blessed be God, blessed be Your most holy name, blessed be the Son of God, Jesus most Holy, etc."

When I ran out of this type of prayer, I looked out my sliding glass door and said, "Thank You God for the trees. Thank You for the grass. Thank You for my chickens. Thank You for that barn, etc."

After I covered all I could see outside I looked around my room and said, "Thank You God for my bed. Thank You for my clothes. Thank You for the mirror, etc."

Soon I exhausted the items of pleasure in my room and began on the negative, "Thank You God for the crack in the ceiling, thank You for the cob-webs in the corners, thank You for the dust on my dresser,..."

Suddenly there was someone standing next to me on my left side. I turned to view him and noticed that my body did not turn, only my spirit. My spirit seemed to look the same as my body and to be the same size. It just moved faster and had more freedom of movement.

The figure next to me had on a long gown and had long hair parted in the middle. His face was just a mist. I could see His hands and hear His voice. He said, "Take the pillow out from under your head."

Well now, I had always slept with a pillow. And here was someone telling me to get rid of it...no way was I going to do this. I said, "Ahhhw Jesus, come on now. You know I've always slept with a pillow under my"... I got no farther. All of a sudden it dawned on me WHO I was arguing with...the God of the universe!

"Yes Sir," I said. And in one single motion, my body as well as my spirit went into action and I pulled that pillow out, passed it over me and sailed it down to land at His feet.

Then He said, "Uncross your feet." Well now, this was going TOO far. I had always lain with my feet crossed. So I said, "Come now, Jesus, You know I have ALWAYS slept with my feet crossed and"... Once more I realized WHO I was fussing at.

"Yes Sir," I said, and quickly uncrossed my feet. At that moment numbness started creeping from my feet up my body.

From the time that Jesus had appeared beside me, there was also a person on the right side of my bed. He had on a black suit, hat and shoes. He himself had a darkness like the nighttime. His smirking, oily voice made me pull away from that side of the bed and I didn't desire to even look at his face. As a cartoon character said in a resent movie, he was "uggggggggggly."

This person kept injecting the words, "You can stop this anytime you want to, you know." As he spoke it felt like my skin crawled. When the numbness started up my body, he said, "Rigormortis is setting in. You are dying, you know."

I turned to Jesus and said, "Whoa, here Lord, let's talk this over." At this point the numbness stopped and waited there. I said, "I bind all spirits that are not of Jesus Christ. God, Your Word says that I have seventy years to live. I'm not seventy. Your Word says You won't deceive me nor allow me to be deceived. If this is not of You God, I don't want it." At this point I heard that same SWEET voice say, "Just trust me"...I did.

The moment I agreed to trust Him, the numbness, that had not gone away, started creeping up my body again. And old-uggggly started his heckling once more. God and I stopped and started every few inches on my body due to my fear and needing God to reassure me that this really WAS Him.

At last the numbness reached my mouth. At that moment a gray oval mist formed at the top of my bedroom wall. Even though Jesus never left my side, He now was coming through the mist with His hand extended, encouraging me to come and join Him. My spirit got up and began floating up to Him as He held securely to my hand. We left the dark, loud-mouth behind.

As we entered the mist it became like a door and we exited out the other side. He took me to visit my Mother. She was on the other side of a great divide but I recognized her old feed-sack print dress. I knew I had to ask her forgiveness. I had taken care of her when she was sick and even helped the nurse care for her when she died at the young age of fifty-three. But I had never forgiven her for some things that happened in my childhood under her care. Then Jesus took me to see my cousin, who had died at the age of eighteen or so. He had embarrassed me in my painful teen years and I had not forgiven him. I asked for his forgiveness.

We started on the journey home to my body. As we passed through the oval mist I heard the most wonderful music. It was coming from everywhere. I couldn't find the source of it.

Jesus stopped at the mist and I traveled downward by myself to enter back into my body. Still looking for the music, my spirit looked down inside my body and saw my heart. It was surrounded by a beautiful kingdom of delicate loveliness...grass, trees etc. In the middle of all this there was my heart standing alone and singing.

It sang, "Father, I adore You. Lay my life before You. How I love You." Then it would sing the second verse, "Jesus I adore You. Lay my life before You. How I love You." When my heart sang the second verse, it would swell out so big that I thought it would literally burst with love. The last verse was for the Spirit and went like the first two. But my heart only expanded on the second verse.

I was so excited. I had read books about the lives of saints when I was a child. In one of them it told of a saint to whom God had given a singing-heart. When I read that, I had asked God to give me one also. Now here I was, all these years later, looking at MY singing heart, just as I had asked. God is so faithful...

But I made a mistake. As the heart would sing, musical notes jumped out of it, float through the air and explode, thus releasing the music...it was stereophonic sound. I was totally fascinated with the notes and looking closely at them I said, "Father God, How do the"...that was as far as I got with my words. One must never question a miracle as to how it comes about. Everything disappeared and I was back to normal.

Once more I could hear the black clothed figure next to me, sounding like a broken record, "You know you can quit this any time you want to."

Being brought back from the world of the spirit so quickly and fearful of the words I was hearing, I jumped straight out of my bed and landed in the middle of the bedroom floor, not having touched a thing along the way.

The heat was gone from my body, the "persons" had disappeared and I had a terrible headache... but, from the neck down I had no pain. For the first time in nine years...I was pain free! GLORY! Jesus had proven that His word is true...He IS the same, yesterday, today and tomorrow.

Chapter 10
SOCIAL SECURITY

Mark 13:5 And Jesus answering them began to say, Take heed lest any [man] deceive you:

Jeremiah 9:5 And they will deceive every one his neighbour, and will not speak the truth: they have taught their tongue to speak lies, [and] weary themselves to commit iniquity.

1 John 3:7 Little children, let no man deceive you: he that doeth righteousness is righteous, even as he is righteous.

Edward had been raised on the streets of Detroit, Michigan. He was small for his age and had to learn street-ways to hold his own. He could do a con-job on people with such a straight face that he could have easily sold refrigerators to igloo dwellers. His specialty was his Social Security Disability check. He like to refer to himself as a "Social Security Baby". He would go to various sales, plan out what he wanted, and then play on the people's sympathy. This got him a reduced rate, money in his pocket, and the confidence to con someone else...until he met Jesus.

Edward and I had left the church we were attending plus the little group of Believers that we studied with each week and had joined a Full Gospel Church that fed us Bible Truths four times a week. We also met in the home of a minister on Saturday nights for some guitar picking, praise reports, and practical discussions of the Christian way of life. Even our druggist laid God's ways on us when we picked up our medicine. And to top all this off, Edward and his best friend discussed Jesus as they visited with each other daily.

This all had a profound effect on Edward and slowly his old life style began to change... but it was very painful for him. I used to say, "Edward, you act like you have a good angel on one of your shoulders and a bad one on the other. And whichever one offers you the best deal is the one you listen to."

Now, I have given these highlights to set the stage for the scenario of "The Death Of The Social Security Baby."

It was the summer after Edward had given his life to Jesus and the yard sales were drawing him like a moth to a flame. He had saved a little money back through the winter in anticipation of wheeling-and-dealing at the various places. He had a long list of the things he needed and not nearly enough savings to buy them with ...thus he resorted to his old street-ways to get what he wanted. I was not aware of the resurrection of the "old" Edward until he came home with his silver-dollar eyes again.

He said, "Dear, you will never guess what God did to me." He then proceeded to tell me how he had checked out a yard sale and found four things he badly needed. Going over to the side yard, he pulled out his money clip, and slipped out his two fifty dollar bills and one five. Then he put a fifty in his left pocket and the other fifty, plus the five, back in the money clip, which he then slid into his right pocket.

Now, Edward was a very meticulous person. He checked everything out two or three times to make sure nothing could go wrong. He assured me that he had double-checked his pockets.

Going up to the man, Edward started telling the man what he needed and added, "..but I am just a poor Social-Security-Baby and don't have but a few dollars. In fact I only have fifty-five dollars and what I want comes to eighty-five dollars. Could I please have these things for that price?" Well, he was so convincing that the man just melted and agreed to the deal.

Edward reached into his pocket and just as he pulled out his money clip the extra fifty dollar bill came out also.

At this point in Edward's story his eyes got even bigger than they first were. He said, "Dear, the Angels moved that bill from my left pocket to my right pocket. Then they caught it up, and as I stood there facing that man, they fluttered that bill around until it landed right down at the man's feet, in full view. Boy, that taught me a lesson. I ain't NEVER going to con anyone again!"

By this time I'm all questions. I said, "Gracious, Edward, what did you do then? What did the man say?"

"Well, I told him I had done this for his own benefit. That he better be more careful. Someday he was going to get ripped off if he went on believing every sob story that people told him."

I was shocked! I said, "Edward, you lied! Don't you realize that the Bible says that all liars will have their part in the lake of fire?" With a big grin on his face, he replied, "Yes, but God is going to deal with me on that... next."

Those whom God loves He rebukes and chasten.

Chapter 11
ATTITUDE CHANGE

Mark 11:25 And when ye stand praying, forgive, if ye have ought against any: that your Father also which is in heaven may forgive you your trespasses.

Luke 17:4 And if he trespass against thee seven times in a day, and seven times in a day turn again to thee, saying, I repent; thou shalt forgive him.

Luke 23:34 Then said Jesus, Father, forgive them; for they know not what they do. And they parted his raiment, and cast lots.

Shortly after Edward and I married, we clashed head-on. It seemed as if nothing suited him...especially me.

In time the Lord united me with a prayer partner in a little village seven miles north of us. Jean and I met through Bible study at our druggist's church. There were so many things I didn't know about God and the Bible, that I was trying to go to all the services I could possibly make at anyone's church.

The topic of teaching was about change. Change your life style. Change your speech. Change your thinking. Change your habits. All I could say to this type of teaching was, "YOU are not married to Edward!"

Jean was her Church's secretary and understood faith inside and out. She began giving me teaching tapes on the latest faith sermons. Then I started calling her to discuss the things I heard on the tapes and this led us into becoming prayer partners. She and I agreed to unite together in prayer about my marriage.

She gave me permission to make unlimited calls for prayer to her daily, at home or work. I made full use of her offer. Coming from a religious background, I had not been trained in any thing but prayers memorized by rote. After I would tell Jean the latest problem I was having, she would launch into the most beautiful prayers I had ever listened to. There was never a memorized prayer among them. I would hang up my phone feeling like I had just been touched some way by heaven.

Depending on Edward's behavior, some days I called Jeanie five or six times. Each time I would give her a blow by blow description of the latest dastardly-deed Edward had pulled on me.

She was the model of patience. Never once did she act like I was a nuisance or that she didn't want to be bothered. She treated me as if I was the most important person in the world. Jean also had come out of a main line religion and understood my hunger to learn and change as much as possible and as fast as I could. When I first started calling, I would end up crying before I finished the latest hurt. As soon as she would pray I would be fine ...until Edward did something else that hurt my feelings.

That poor lady heard the same problems, but in different settings, so many times, she could have recited the problems from memory.

The most amazing thing about Jean was the fact that she NEVER said a negative thing about Edward. As she counseled me before she prayed, she just kept reminding me who our real enemy on this earth is...and it wasn't Edward.

As she kept lifting us up in prayer something in me began to change. I tired of hearing myself complain about hurt feelings. I began to realize that Satan, our enemy, was using Edward to steal my joy of living. Poor Edward was as much a victim as I was. When I first started calling Jean, I didn't realize this and blamed Edward as my joy-killer.

My calls to her went like this, "Oh Jean, let me tell you what Edward just did.. .sniff. .sniff...He was etc, etc." And I would go on and on for an hour with the appropriate tears to match.

As I started to learn more about Kingdom living, my calls went like this, "Jean, that dirty rat did it again, let me tell...no, forget it. I've told you before. I just need you to pray." I had stopped crying over every little hurt.

Many tapes and phone calls later I started my calls like this, "It's me, Jeanie, just pray."

And finally, my rare calls would go like this, "Hi, Jeanie, what's new with you?"

I had gotten the victory over the enemy, my flesh, uncontrolled emotions and old programming.

Finally I understood what God had been trying to teach me through this. Edward wasn't seeking God with an unquenchable thirst..I was. Edward didn't change..I did. Edward was satisfied with the natural life...I wasn't.

God had made Matthew 5:6 a reality in my life....Blessed are they which do hunger and thirst after righteousness: for they shall be filled.

Chapter 12
THE BAR

1 Thessalonians 4:7 For God hath not called us unto uncleanness, but unto holiness.

Colossians 3:5 Mortify therefore your members which are upon the earth; fornication, uncleanness, inordinate affection, evil concupiscence, and covetousness, which is idolatry:

1 Corinthians 6:19 What? know ye not that your body is the temple of the Holy Ghost [which is] in you, which ye have of God, and ye are not your own?

When I came out of the religion that I had depended on from my youth, I was angry at God. I blamed Him for all the troubles in my life. So, for four years I lived wild and reckless. To put it bluntly, I lived a life of sin. I met Edward during this time in my life and later we were married.

The pre-nuptial agreement we made was to live our marriage by the Bible. Neither of us knew exactly what this meant but we were willing to learn. We started by attending a denomination that was new to us both.

The next step was joining with three couples and meeting in each others homes once a week. It was in this group that we learned what real worship was and the importance of the Bible in our daily lives.

In time we settled down in a Full Gospel Church and it became the center of our lives. Anything it offered we took part in. We began to pray together in the mornings and evenings. The Bible taught us to replace our old harmful pastimes with constructive things and as we did this, we slowly began to change. Learning new ways was hard and painful, especially for me.

In the past when someone did me a wrong, I had suffered silently, never voicing my hurts or anger. In time the doctors had encouraged me to stop this way of coping with stresses or I would lose my physical health, which had already suffered a great deal from this type of coping. So I went into marriage with Edward determined to hold my own by talking things out.

Edward had a fault that didn't show up until after we were married. He had a way of tormenting someone until that someone wanted to gun-him-down at high-noon.

I was an only child, grew up in a neighborhood where there weren't any children and my mother spent most of her time in bed, reading books. God, my father and the neighbors raised me. I was always lonely and the height of my life was when grown-ups came to visit with their children.

Being an only child, I never learned the art of arguing, acting selfish with others, or holding my own in a fight. And to just torment someone was more than I could understand.

So when Edward started his childish tormenting, I would set him down and try to discuss why he was being so obnoxious. This got us nowhere. It seemed as if these moods of his just had to wear themselves out.

The trouble was I would wear out before the moods would. Then all that inward anger I had kept in check would explode and I would throw a temper fit. We didn't argue because I didn't let him get a word in edgewise. I just simply yelled and screamed at him until I ran out of breath and things to say.

God was dealing with us on this. He was trying to teach us a better way. But I was a slow learner in this area and my husband was slower. With the help of a prayer partner I finally caught on, but until I did, marriage was a real struggle for us.

The second year we were married, the time came that Edward had tormented me for days. One night, halfway into the second week of his foolishness, I had endured enough and was determined to get even. Grabbing my coat, and heading to the door, I screamed at him, "I can't stand you any longer. I'm going in town to the bar and let the men admire me."

I had worked as a waitress at a dinner and dance lounge the summer before we met. People would tell me that I was not the average bar-girl type, since I didn't imbibe in strong drink or date any of the customers nor use coarse language around them. This, of course, only intrigued the clientele more then if I did do these things. It brought me quite a few admirers. They would feed my ego, while I sat quietly and sipped cokes.

On the night that I was heading to town to get even, I was telling the Lord all that was wrong with Edward. I never once mentioned anything about the wrong I was intending to do when I got to town.

Halfway to town, something heavy fell on me. It was nothing visible, just an extreme tiredness. My head felt like it was to heavy to hold up. I said, "Wow, Lord, I didn't realize I was so tired. I'm not going to town, I'm going back home."

Approaching our house I saw Edward's truck next to the front door and anger surged up again. The tiredness left me. I said, "Lord, I am going to my prayer partner's house and tell her how rotten Edward is."

Once more I got half way to where I was going and the heaviness fell on me. Feeling bushed, I turned around and headed home the second time.

As I neared the house just the sight of Edward's truck up on our hill stirred my anger once more. Tiredness flew right out my car window. I said, "Lord, I'm going to go to his best friend's house and tell them how terrible Edward is...they think he is so wonderful."

I sped pass the house and made the turn off on two wheels. Half way to his friend's house, you guessed it, the heaviness was back. "Ok, God I give up. I am going home."I was careful to not look at Edward's truck this time.

When I walked into the house, Edward was still sitting in the same place I had left him thirty-some minutes ago.

As I walked to the closet I threw a, "Forgive me for screaming at you," over my shoulder. "But I'm only asking because God says I have to." Edward looked up at me with such a sad look on his face I was shocked. He said, "I'm sorry I have been so terrible. I was praying for you to come home." Now Edward wasn't the praying type. He made me do all the praying.

I looked down at him and said, "You were praying that I would come home?" A light-ray of knowledge was beginning to come on. I was remembering that unusual tiredness that had fallen on me three times. I said, "Edward, how many times did you pray that I would come home?"

"Three times," he answered.

Well, once more, God had showed himself strong in our behalf. He is in the marriage saving business. Needless to say, I was cured of even THINKING about going to the bar for any reason.

Chapter 13
THE JAR

Proverbs 6:2 Thou art snared with the words of thy mouth, thou art taken with the words of thy mouth.

Proverbs 12:13 The wicked is snared by the transgression of [his] lips: but the just shall come out of trouble.

Isaiah 28:13 But the word of the LORD was unto them precept upon precept, precept upon precept; line upon line, line upon line; here a little, [and] there a little; that they might go, and fall backward, and be broken, and snared, and taken.

God began to deal with my husband and me about the words that came out of our mouths. The scripture of James 3:10 kept popping up everywhere..."Out of the same mouth proceedeth blessings and cursings. My brethren, these things ought not so to be."

Cursing to some people, (and to Edward and me,) consisted of only taking God's name in vain, but when I began to read the Bible closer I saw in Mark 11:21 where Jesus cursed the fig tree. Well, He didn't use God's name to do that. He only said, "No man shall eat fruit of thee hereafter for ever."

I began to understand a spiritual principle here. Anything that is not encouraging or on the positive side causes things or people to malfunction...it becomes a curse to them. No wonder Jesus had cautioned us in Matthew 5:22 not to call anyone a fool. In Greek, the word fool means dull, stupid, heedless, blockhead, or absurd.

Edward and I thought back to the time before the Holy Spirit came into our lives. We had been raised on these words at home, at school, through books and finally television. To a lesser degree we spoke these same words to our children and had allowed the use of them by our children. Since this was a natural way of life for us, I could feel in my bones that we were in for some heavy battles with our old programming.

For a while we worked at changing, but the going was slow and we weren't really committed. One Sunday an Evangelist came to our church and taught on "Getting control of our mouths." She explained how she and her husband had changed the negative words they had been raised on, to nothing but life-giving words.

They had each gotten a bottle and put their names on them. Every time one of them said a dirty or a negative word, they had to drop a nickel in their respective bottles. Her husband had been in the military service and he constantly spiced his everyday conversations with four letter words. With their game-plan in force they cleaned up their act in no time at all.

I went home armed with determination to change. I got our bottles, put our names on them, and set the starting time for seven a.m. the next morning. After considering our finances and our mouths we decided to start with pennies instead of nickels, but to spice up the game a little, I decided we would give our bottles to one another at the end of each week. This was a mistake on my part.

With the challenge of swapping jars, Edward set out to win mine. And of course, a near empty jar had no appeal for him, therefore he methodically baited me so I would say negative words. Being of Irish descent, and quick with a come-back, my jar was soon full. When the week was up, I painfully handed over TWO FILLED JARS.

For Edward, an empty jar was easy since he didn't talk much to start with. So to win, he just completely shut up, but to keep me from catching on to his strategy, he sat around looking at me with love-sick eyes and smiling constantly. This worked for a while, due to the fact that big talkers rarely notice if another is verbalizing...

In time, I realized that he was setting me up. I was furious, and wordy, which naturally cost me more pennies...but that became my turning point. The pain of humiliation helped me overcome my choice of words and the day finally came when I handed Edward seven measly pennies for one whole week.

It is now fifteen years later, and the lesson I learned from my penny jar is still with me. When I am with other Christians and I hear the negative words, put downs, four letter words, and self-condemnation, I feel so sad for them. They are bringing curses down on themselves and those around them and they don't even realize it.

At the same time I praise Our Lord for the lessons and discipline He taught me through the rigged penny jar.

Also, I now listen to other people to see if they are just indulging me, or if they are self-starters in conversations. I have tried to slow my mouth down so I can act and not react to statements and situations around me.

I still slip up now and then but if Edward were still alive today, my penny jar would not be lucrative enough to engage him into playing the "game."

God disciplines those He loves.

Chapter 14
TITHE

Malachi 3:10 Bring ye all the tithes into the storehouse, that there may be meat in mine house, and prove me now herewith, saith the LORD of hosts, if I will not open you the windows of heaven, and pour you out a blessing, that [there shall] not [be room] enough [to receive it].

Malachi 3:11 And I will rebuke the devourer for your sakes, and he shall not destroy the fruits of your ground; neither shall your vine cast her fruit before the time in the field, saith the LORD

Matthew 23:23 Woe unto you, scribes and Pharisees, hypocrites! for ye pay tithe of mint and anise and cummin, and have omitted the weightier [matters] of the law, judgment, mercy, and faith: these ought ye to have done, and not to leave the other undone.

Our druggist, Brother Bob, began teaching Edward and me about tithing the Bible way. It sounded good..but, we were not sure it would work for us.

Edward was drawing a Social Security check, plus a Veterans check, when we met. After we were married, the V.A. cut their check off, leaving us only the S.S. check to live on.

Talk about being between a rock and a hard place, we were there. To add to this hardship, Brother Bob was trying to tell us that we would GAIN if we gave God ten percent of what little we had.

We debated the pros and cons of this system. Brother Bob tithed and he did have all his needs met, just like the Bible said he would. This was a pro...but, Brother Bob had his health, an excellent paying profession, and his youth.

We finally decided to give God's Word a try in this area. Everything else we had tried had worked...maybe this would also. I sat down to make out the bills and tithing went first place on the list. With a little trimming and careful eating we managed to pay our bills that month...but the next month wasn't that easy. No matter how I figured everything, I just could not pay the necessary bills and tithe.

I laid our dilemma before God, "God, we will be delighted to pay our ten percent when You supply it for us. You say we are supposed to owe no man anything...but to fulfill this, we need the Veterans Disability check that was cut off. We are waiting on You."

With no prompting on our part, two weeks after the prayer, the Veterans Administration wrote to us. They had decided to reinstate Edward's Veterans Administration's benefits, and even raise them since he was now married.

I quickly sat down to figure up how this extra money would affect our budget. I started with the ten percent tithe on the S.S. check that we needed. I added to this the ten percent tithe on the V.A. check that we would be getting. Next, I deducted the extra income from our food stamps and figured that food cost with the tithe amount of the Veteran's check. The final results left us with everything paid, including the old tithe and the new tithe...and not one dime left over.

God had indeed supplied the tithing money we had asked Him for. But He also had made sure we had enough to pay it on the added check and had even taken our food stamp reduction into consideration.

Once more Brother Bob was right..."God is faithful to His Word."

Chapter 15
$500.00

James 2:16 And one of you say unto them, Depart in peace, be [ye] warmed and filled; notwithstanding ye give them not those things which are needful to the body; what [doth it] profit?

2 Corinthians 9:7 Every man according as he purposeth in his heart, [so let him give]; not grudgingly, or of necessity: for God loveth a cheerful giver.

Luke 6:38 Give, and it shall be given unto you; good measure, pressed down, and shaken together, and running over, shall men give into your bosom. For with the same measure that ye mete withal it shall be measured to you again.

Our house was centrally located between two little towns in Michigan. Our church was in one town and our pharmacy was in the other. It was the pharmacy that I most looked forward to visiting.

Our druggist and his family were wonderful Christians and I was learning so much from them. We had a common bond that no one could break. We had left the same religious denomination and joined up with the same Spirit-Led denomination. We had been grafted together by the Blood of Jesus and we understood one another. We were family by God's adoption plan.

Brother Bob became the big brother I never had and I hung on his every word. He loved Jesus like I loved Jesus. At the mere telling of a miracle, Brother Bob would get all teary eyed and have to clear his throat. Sometimes he couldn't even talk, other times he made a squeaky sound like a rusty door makes when forced to open. I loved it. This was a spiritual drink for my parched spirit.

I used any excuse I could to go to the drug store. Once there, Brother Bob and I would swap stories about Jesus. Since he was the owner as well as the pill-filler, we could get by with this. It was he, in between waiting on customers, that taught my husband and me about tithing.

When Edward and I first started going there Brother Bob had not been in business very long and customers were sparse. Along with myself, Brother Bob's pastor came in the store often, so we had a lot of teaching and question time.

After a few months, things began to change. Pastor got busier and Brother Bob and I settled for less teaching and more miracle-stories. Then another change came about. As soon as we would start telling miracle-stories, it seemed like people were coming out of the woodwork...there would be customers everywhere. Sometimes we would have to finish a story on another visit, because the whole store resembled busy Wal-Mart at Christmas time...God was blessing.

During this time, Edward and I were struggling to make ends meet. We were tithing like the Bible and Brother Bob taught us, but it seemed like as we took one step forward we would slip two steps back. I finally made a list of the monthly payments of our bills and posted it on the wall above the kitchen table. As we joined in prayer and Bible reading each morning, we would lift this list up to God and ask Him to pay it. Edward went along with this...but he really thought I had lost my mind.

One morning, around income tax time, Brother Bob called and asked if he and his wife could come over for tea...they would bring the cookies. Even though I loved this family dearly, they had never been to our house. We were family only in Jesus...not socially. "Hummmmm", I said, "What are you up to, God?"

After tea time, as we sat around the table, Brother Bob pulled out a long, white envelope and handed it to me. He said, "The Lord told me that we should share our profits with you, so here is your half." I gave the envelope to Edward. As he started to open it and money began to pop up, Edward looked scared and throwing the envelope down on the table said, "You open it." There was five hundred dollars in the package.

I said to Edward, "This is the answer to our prayers about our bills." "No, this is for the house taxes," he countered. I said,

"Tell you what, Love, let me figure up the bills. If it comes within one dollar, more or less, of the amount to pay off these bills, not to just make a payment, it is for them. If not, we pay the taxes, even though taxes are eight hundred, not five." We agreed.

On Monday I called each company and asked for the amount of the balance that we owed them. By the time we deducted tithing moneys, we were exactly one dollar over the five hundred dollars.

The Bible says that if we lift up Jesus, God will draw all men unto Him. It is the Spirit of God that does the work. He only needs our bodies, and cooperation. It was He that prospered Brother Bob's store, as Brother and I lifted up Jesus, and it was He that was now prospering Edward and me through our Brother. God is faithful.

Chapter 16
DEER SEASON

Mark 9:23 Jesus said unto him, If thou canst believe, all things [are] possible to him that believeth.

Mark 11:24 Therefore I say unto you, What things soever ye desire, when ye pray, believe that ye receive [them], and ye shall have [them].

Hebrews 11:6 But without faith [it is] impossible to please [him]: for he that cometh to God must believe that he is, and [that] he is a rewarder of them that diligently seek him.

In the religion that Edward and I were raised in, we were never taught about tithing. No one told us that God wants us to tithe, so we can receive. We always thought it was a get rich system, devised by greedy men, for their own benefit. Brother Bob, the druggist, helped us to see differently.

One winter, right before hunting season, Edward went to Brother Bob's store and said, "I want you to agree with us in prayer that I will get a deer during the coming season."

Brother Bob was more than happy to agree with Edward in prayer for a deer. Since it was he that had encouraged Edward to start tithing, he used tithing as the basis for Edward's prayer request.

Normally, Edward went with some old hunting buddies on the first day of the season. But this particular year a neighbor from two farms away asked if he could go hunting with Edward the first day. He had not been hunting since he was 16 years old and he didn't want to go alone. So Edward decided that just the two of us would go hunting with this young man.

Opening day of hunting season, the three of us gathered around our table and started our day with a prayer. Edward prayed that God would give the young man a deer, and we all agreed with the request. I added to the prayer, " And please, God, let the deer just walk out in front of this young man's gun."

When we got to Edward's happy hunting grounds, Edward decided to let the young man use his very own, private, sacred, one-of-a-kind, deer blind. We staked ourselves out further up the hill. At six o'clock sharp we heard the sound of a gun shot from the deer blind. Edward waited for the traditional hunter's second shot which meant it was all over. The moment we heard it, Edward took off for the blind, shouting, "He got it!"

Sure enough, there lay a buck...the large-rack buck that Edward had been trying to get for himself. One look at that deer, and Edward started grieving, "The kid got my deer. He was in my deer blind, using my gun, and that is the deer I have been stalking for years." There was no consoling Edward. Not even when I mentioned the fact that the young man told us the deer had just walked out in front of his gun and stood there like we had prayed.

Of course, the young man didn't ease my husband's pain any. Not knowing of Edward's sorrow, he tied the deer on top of his car and drove up and down the roads all day showing it off to everyone. Each trip brought him past our picture window where Edward sat grieving.

On top of all this, the young man asked Edward to help him dress out his deer, since he knew nothing about butchering and wrapping. The two of us butchered, wrapped and gave the wife cooking lessons on "How To Make Deer Taste Like Beef." The young man gave us a gift of a deer steak for helping him.

Edward and I went hunting every day for the rest of that week, and never even saw another deer. The second week, Edward headed to Brother Bob's for a confrontation, "I thought you said that God would give me a deer." To which the Druggist replied, "He will Edward. We agreed and you are a tither. God is faithful, just be patient." For the rest of the season, Edward made extra trips to the Drug Store...trying to get Brother Bob to admit that there was no deer for Edward.

Hunting season came and went. Edward was deerless. He was still making his weekly trip to the Drug Store to remind the Druggist about his deer. Each week Brother Bob would patiently explain to Edward that he would get his deer, because God was faithful and Edward was a tither.

Spring came, and the young man had his hogs butchered. Well, if there was anything that Edward liked better than deer meat, it was hog meat. The young man called to ask me if Edward would like some and what kind did he like. To which I replied, "Yes, he would like some and he likes anything except the hooves and eyeballs." He blessed us with a ham, some bacon, pork chops and homemade sausage.

You would think that all that pork, and the one deer steak, would have brought peace to Edward's heart...it didn't! He was still reminding Brother Bob on a regular basis that God had not answered that prayer yet.

Months went by. One day I got another phone call from the young neighbor who went hunting with us. He said, "My wife and I are going to move back to town and we won't be keeping the deep freeze. My wife didn't like the deer meat so we still have it all, except for the one piece we gave to you and the one she tried. Do you think Edward would want the rest of it?"

So, the deer season finally ended for Edward and the Druggist. Brother Bob had been right all along...God is faithful.

Chapter 17
TEACH

Exodus 4:12 Now therefore go, and I will be with thy mouth, and teach thee what thou shalt say.

2 Timothy 2:2 And the things that thou hast heard of me among many witnesses, the same commit thou to faithful men, who shall be able to teach others also.

Acts 5:42 And daily in the temple, and in every house, they ceased not to teach and preach Jesus Christ.

From the day I met the Holy Spirit of God I began to pour over the Bible with an unquenchable thirst. I wanted to know all I could about my heritage as a Christian and in time, eight study hours a day were as two hours spent with my Beloved Lord. I had not yet read the verse from Luke 12:48, ".....for unto whomsoever much is given, of him shall be much required:..."

The day of Luke 12:48 finally arrived for me. I knew I was to teach others what I was learning. I started giving God reason after reason why I could not teach. As God shot down each excuse I gave Him, I began to grow a little bolder and at last I agreed to try. But the question was, "Whom would I teach?" Every Christian around me knew more than I did about the Bible. Finally I asked my friend, who had grown up in Kentucky as I had, if I could come over and practice on her...she agreed.

On the way to her house, reality set in and I said, "God, this is not going to work. You know I am fine on a one-to-one basis. If I am going to learn to teach I need more people there than just my friend, Beulah, but I am too scared to ask anyone else to come." It seemed to me that what God was asking of me was so beyond my ability that I just sat in the car and cried.

You see, I had been born with a learning disability and I read words backward. I often talked backwards and would have been a great hit in Mexico with my adjectives spoken after my nouns. In my school-days the teachers and fellow classmates didn't understand about such things. So, students like me were subject to much ridicule and the weak at heart dropped out of school while the strong ones learned to clown their way through. Due to my strict Father, I chose to clown.

Now here I was in my middle years, with only a G.E.D. to my credit and very little confidence in my learning ability being called by God to go teach. All I could say was, "God, you sure do have a sense of humor."

Beulah knew just how to make someone like me feel accepted. She was waiting at her door with open arms, smiles, lots of love and ushered me into the living room to get started.

As I opened our Bible class with prayer, I felt impressed upon by the Holy Spirit to ask for angels to attend our meeting. After all, the Bible says in 1 Peter 1:12, "...which things the angels desire to look into." Maybe they could learn something, for I knew in my heart, Beulah wouldn't.

It was the dead of winter in Boyne City, Michigan, and my friend was using one small wood burning stove to heat the whole house. It did very little when it was as cold as it was that day. Just as I finished the opening prayer, the room we were in became so hot I assumed that Beulah had gotten up during the prayer and put wood in the stove, even though I didn't hear any movement. Raising my head and opening my eyes, I looked into what appeared to be the faces of my friends and fellow church members sitting around the room. Their bodies and faces were hazy but distinguishable. I began to talk to each one as if they were really there in their bodies.

The room was so full of angels that I kept thinking of the joke, "How many angels can stand on the head of a pin." They were stacked up to the ceiling in the back of the room...as if they were sitting on bleachers at a ball game.

Panic began to set in when I reached for my notes only to find I had left them at home. My mind went blank and I shot a quick prayer to God for help. It was as if He said, "It's o.k." So I just opened the Bible at random and started to read. As I turned the page, I looked over to the margin and there was the cue-verse that I needed for the study I had prepared. Just as for Abraham,

God had provided the "..ram in the bush." (Gen. 22:13) Through all of this I was as calm as if nothing out of the ordinary was happening.

The study came to a close and I ended in a prayer of rejoicing for all that God had done. The instant I said, "..amen.", the room became freezing cold. I looked up and no one was there but Beulah, me... and a cold stove. The fire had died out and neither of us had known it. How right our pastor had been when he said, "Whom God calls, He qualifies." God had been faithful again.

Chapter 18
FIRE

Hebrews 2:15 And deliver them who through fear of death were all their lifetime subject to bondage.

2 Timothy 1:7 For God hath not given us the spirit of fear; but of power, and of love, and of a sound mind.

Luke 12:7 But even the very hairs of your head are all numbered. Fear not therefore: ye are of more value than many sparrows.

My husband was such a worrier. If things were going badly, he would worry. If things were going good he would worry. He would even wake up at night worried because he wasn't worried.

Pastor and our druggist were trying to teach Edward that God would take care of everything in our life, if we would just replace worry with faith. I used to tell him, "Edward, you have more faith in what the devil can do than you have faith in what God can overcome."

We had begun to have a Bible class at our house on Monday nights. I was teaching as fast as I was learning and Edward was my best student... on Monday nights. The rest of the week "WORRIER-ED" was back.

When he was little the house he lived in had caught on fire which he had never gotten over. No one was hurt, but the possibilities of what could have happened never left him. This caused him to constantly worry that our stove would catch on fire and burn us up in our sleep.

One day I came in the house and Edward was installing a water pipe, with an off and on spigot in our hall closet. I said, "Edward, what in the world are you doing?"

He said, "I can't sleep at night. I keep thinking the wood stove will catch on fire and we will burn up, so I'm installing a water system here next to the stove. We'll have regular fire drills, so we will know what to do if a fire does start."

Sure enough, Edward had a garden hose all curled up and attached to the water faucet he had installed. The hose had an attachment on the other end to make water pressure and the water valve was on and operating. This was our new fire-killer system.

We began our practice drills. Now secretly, I was beginning to doubt Edward's sanity, but like the good little wife, I went along with his plans, always qualifying the whole scenario with, "God will take care of us, Love. This really isn't necessary."

Then one day, I stumbled on to a Bible truth in Job 3:25

that changed my way of thinking in a lot of areas. It said, "The things Job feared, came upon him." Wow! This explained a lot of things that had happened to me in my lifetime.

My mother was worse than Edward about fear and worry. As I grew up, she passed quite a number of her fears on to me. And as I looked back, I could see that those were the areas of my life that I had trouble in. A new day was dawning for me...but, not for Edward. Even with the new fire-department installed in our closet, he still was worried about a fire.

The day finally came...fire struck. A man knocked on our door and told us our chimney was on fire. Precious Edward forgot all he had practiced for the last few months. He started running around the living room yelling, "Dear, what are we going to do? What are we going to do?"

I couldn't believe my eyes. He had gone bonkers...flipped-out. The thing that he feared had come upon him. He finally had a fire and he had mentally skipped town. I took his hand and said, "Let's pray, Edward."

"Oh yeah," he said. After a VERY short prayer, Edward came to himself, ran for his water hose and said, "Open the stove door so I can put out the fire."

I said, " Edward, if you turn THAT hose into THAT stove, we won't be able to start a fire in there for the rest of the winter. Let's just shut the damper on the stove pipe and let it smother itself out." We did...and it did.

About three hours later, Edward was just sitting on the couch thinking...this usually spelled trouble in the worry-department. Finally he looked up and said, "You know something Dear, I'm glad that stove caught on fire. Now I don't have to worry about it any more. And you were right...God will take care of us."

I wish I could say that this was the last of Edward's sleepless nights. But it wasn't. He just didn't worry about fire anymore.

I'm glad God once lived on this earth just like us. It gives me a good feeling to know He understands all our peculiarities.

Chapter 19
TEMPER

Colossians 3:8 But now ye also put off all these; anger, wrath, malice, blasphemy, filthy communication out of your mouth.

Proverbs 16:32 [He that is] slow to anger [is] better than the mighty; and he that ruleth his spirit than he that taketh a city.

Proverbs 15:1 A soft answer turneth away wrath: but grievous words stir up anger.

Anger is a thing that I have always struggled with. When I was young, I learned quickly that temper-tantrums could not be thrown in my family...yet, no one demonstrated a sensible way to deal with the anger that causes them.

When I answered the call to follow in the footsteps of Jesus, God began to deal with me about my unbridled emotions. This was a time of change and pain for me. I will share with you one of the incidents of my suffering.

I was teaching Bible classes in four villages around us, plus in our home. I tried to instill in the students some of the responsibilities of being a Christian...one of them being to be on time wherever we go. It looks bad for the Kingdom of God, that we represent, when we run late, hold others up, or miss part of what we have come to hear...it has to do with respect of others.

Due to what I was teaching, I was always on time, and sometimes early, so I could set a good example. Well, the day finally came when I couldn't produce. I had gotten into my car and it wouldn't start, but Edward was still home, so he started it for me and said, "I have to get you a new battery."

The next morning the same thing happened and Edward wasn't there. So, I prayed, "Lord, I need to get this car started. Help me, please." A friend came by just then and jump-started my car. God had supplied and I was happy.

The next day, once again my car refused to start. Confidently, I prayed, "Lord, send me someone to start my car." I waited, but no one came. I prayed again, "Lord, you know how I always teach the students to be on time. It will look bad if You don't help me and I run late. Do something, please."

I waited, but again nothing happened. I laid hands on the dash board, and prayed the prayer for healing. I waited...the car stayed sick.

During this time, my anger began to manifest itself. My stomach started to tighten up in a tight little knot, my hands began stroking my forehead, my teeth clenched together, my eyes began to squint, and some very un-christian thoughts were trying to form in my mind. To state it simple, I was getting VERY annoyed with God for not listing to me.

Finally, old-faithful erupted once more. I jumped out of my car, and with a fierce temper-fit and a clenched fist, I yelled at God, "all right! all right! I can't go now. And it is all Your fault. You could have helped me but You didn't. Now it's too late to drive the thirty-five miles to class. I would be late and I can't be late myself and teach others not to be." Then I let out a very loud, "EEERRRRRhhh!!!"

With that final outburst, I slammed the car door, kicked the fender, and limped toward the house, fussing at God all the way.

I called the hostess of our classes and started to explain that I couldn't make it. She stopped me with a loud, "Wonderful!"

I held the phone away from me and just looked at it, trying to figure out if there was something wrong with our connection. The lady's reaction to my not coming was out of character for her.

Her explanation went like this, "All of the students canceled for today. (A whole living room full) And my sister-in-law just called and wanted me to go shopping down-state with her. I told her I couldn't because you were already on your way here. Now I can go!" To say I was embarrassed would be putting it mildly. I got off that phone so humbled that a worm could not have crawled under my belly. I knelt down in my kitchen, and with tears in my eyes I begged God to forgive me and help me to get rid of this ungodly behavior that I had been cursed with all my life.

I then laid down on the floor and cried like my heart would break.........and something in me did break. It was the childhood-programming's power-hold over my emotions. From that point on until today I have steadily gotten better at dealing with situations that are not to my liking.

When I realized that God had everything under control that day, for my good and His Glory, it was awesome to me. He was saving me an unnecessary thirty-mile trip, answering the prayers of the lady who really wanted to go shopping, and keeping the car home to be repaired.

The most amazing thing about this whole scenario was that the love of God and His forgiveness came pouring into me while I lay there on that floor. If God were like us, He would harbor resentment toward me for such an outburst. He would never forget it. And of course, He would tell everyone in heaven, "...she was just terrible to Me, when I was only trying to help her."

Wow! I'm sure glad that Isaiah 55:8 is true. "For my thoughts are not your thoughts, neither are your ways my ways, saith the Lord." Someday I shall be like Him...He promised!

Chapter 20
CLOTHES

2 Corinthians 8:14 But by an equality, [that] now at this time your abundance [may be a supply] for their want, that their abundance also may be [a supply] for your want: that there may be equality:

Philippians 4:19 But my God shall supply all your need according to his riches in glory by Christ Jesus.

1 John 3:17 But whoso hath this world's good, and seeth his brother have need, and shutteth up his bowels [of compassion] from him, how dwelleth the love of God in him?

Philippians 4:19 says, "But my God shall supply all your need according to his riches in glory by Christ Jesus." To supply for us is God's job. Our job is to believe it. Hummmmmm....God got the easy part.

Living on a fixed-income keeps one from going about naked, homeless or starving, but it sure doesn't allow for any frills. Being a female, I do go in for frills...especially new clothes. So I regularly made the rounds of the yard sales, thrift stores and church rummage sales looking for frills.

Now that I had started teaching Bible classes, I just had to have better clothes than my wardrobe held. Now and then, I would happen on to a really good-buy, but for the most part, it was just what the signs said... rubbish..oops..ha, ha,...rummage.

As I was teaching on Philippians 4:19 one day, suddenly I came alive to the words, "..all your need". Well, clothes were certainly a NEED for me. Some of mine were ten years old and mostly thread bare. Yes, I did need clothes. As I read on, more words caught hold of me..."according to His riches in glory". Well now, here was something I had not noticed before. My clothes..er..ha, ha,..MY NEED..did not have to be according to what I could afford. It had absolutely nothing to do with our fixed-income. It was according to HIS riches in glory.

"Hummmm," I said, "If God wears clothes, I am sure they aren't threadbare. I'll bet He doesn't have holes in the soles of His shoes like I have. Why, come to think of it, even the streets of the new Jerusalem are to be paved with gold. His riches makes our riches look like poverty-row, even if we are millionaires." Ah, ha! Now I was getting somewhere.

I went home and got busy making signs...one for my closet, and one for the kitchen cabinets. I printed the Bible verse in big bold letters that I could see across the room without my glasses and then I hung them up.

Edward came in from the garage, took one look around, and rolled his eyes skyward. I said, "Edward, God said it, I believe it, and that makes it so, for me. Laugh all you want, but He WILL supply."

Every time I went by the signs, I would say the words out loud. Then I would thank God for taking care of my need, even though it had not materialized yet.

Several weeks passed. One day I got a phone call. It was from my prayer partner. Her husband had died years before, and had left her well-fixed financially. This gal had class...wore the best clothes, shopped in the best stores, owned a gorgeous home, had plans for a new home overlooking her lake, and had MY taste in clothes.

We prayed together daily on the phone, but this time she wasn't like herself. Something was up. After a few moments of chit-chat, Jean said, "Lee, our Heavenly Father told me that I should divide my clothes with you. So...can you come over to my house? I want you to pick out half of all the clothes I have in my closet." After the first shock wave passed from me, I did my usual miracle thing...I screamed.

As I carried in arm loads of clothes, just my size, just my taste, and just my colors, I said to Edward, "It sure pays to take God at His word, doesn't it, Love?"

Now, some of you "Doubting-Toms" may say, "She knew you and felt sorry for you. That wasn't God." My reply to that is this..."I knew lots of other people who also KNEW me, but they didn't offer any clothes. And if she just felt sorry for me why did it take her so LONG to feel sorry for me? Why didn't she give them to me BEFORE I started to stand on God's Word for clothes?????" Gotcha!

God is Faithful.

Chapter 21
$50.00

Romans 10:8 But what saith it? The word is nigh thee, [even] in thy mouth, and in thy heart: that is, the word of faith, which we preach;

Proverbs 15:23 A man hath joy by the answer of his mouth: and a word [spoken] in due season, how good [is it]!

Psalms 119:172 My tongue shall speak of thy word: for all thy commandments [are] righteousness.

Shortly after God replenished my wardrobe, Edward and I were faced with a real dilemma. Something unusual had come up that affected our budget. So, after we paid the usual living expenses, we only had half of our allotted grocery moneys left for the whole month. We decided that this was an ideal setting for a miracle.

Having placed an eight by ten inch sign of Philippians 4:19 on the refrigerator door, I quoted it out loud every time I passed by the kitchen. But needing something more, I sat down and made out my grocery list, estimating everything would cost about fifty dollars. I raised the list toward God and said, "Lord, Philippians 4:19 says you will supply all our needs according to your riches in Glory through Christ Jesus. We need fifty dollars for groceries."

Each day, as I ran out of things, I would add them to my list. Then I would remind God of His Word and the fifty dollars. At the beginning of the third week, we were starting to draw in our belts.

When the third week ended, I sat down and cried as if my heart would break. I said, "Lord, I want to remind you of something. You said you would supply all my need according to your riches in glory...but you haven't. I even made out a list so you would know what I need. I have quoted your word out loud and defended you to everyone. But so far, you haven't come through with it. I NEED that fifty dollars. I don't know what else to do."

Just then a Sister from our church whom I knew only slightly called me on the phone. She could tell something was wrong and started asking questions. I finally burst out crying and told her all about the list, the sign, the fifty dollars, and our quickly shrinking food supply. I ended up with the explanation, "It isn't me I am concerned about. I can eat peanut butter and jelly for a couple weeks, but Edward can't because he is a diabetic and has to have certain foods."

She began to ask what was on my list. I told her a couple items until I realized that she was writing them down. I said, "No! I don't want you to bring me food. I asked God for fifty dollars and I expect Him to supply."

She began trying to soothe me with statements like, "God often works through people...it doesn't necessarily have to be fifty dollars as long as you get the food you need...etc, etc." I quit listening because she just didn't understand that it was the principle of the thing as well as the food.

Shortly after she hung up, there was a knock on our door and standing outside was the lady and her husband. He was holding a large box in his arms. They had filled it with all the things I had on my list and some extra, even though I had only told her a couple items. The only thing missing was a loaf of bread and some butter, but I didn't tell her that.

After church that night, a Christian Sister we barely knew invited us to her house for coffee. She loved to bake and she served us two kinds of her home made bread.

As we started to leave she said, "Oh, by the way, my son will be gone for awhile and I baked bread before I knew he wouldn't be here. Would you mind if I give you two some of this bread so it won't go to waste?"

As she pulled it out of the refrigerator she said, "And of course, bread is not good without butter. I'll put in some of that also." My list was complete.

Now, I can't say I wasn't grateful to God for seeing us through...I was. But, at the same time I was disappointed. Pastor had just taught us to be specific with God about our needs and I had done that...I had asked for fifty dollars. You can't get any more specific than that...but it hadn't come. Lack of gratitude was Not my problem. It was the principle of the thing. Is God binding to His Word, or isn't He?

Three more weeks passed and once again we were short on groceries, due to those unexpected expenses the month before. Each day I reminded God about our shortfall and as I did, I would also ask Him what happen to my fifty dollars.

A couple of days into the fourth week I got a phone call from one of the young men of our church. He had just gotten back from down-state and wanted to come and visit with us.

After he arrived, and settled in, this is the story he told us. "Last month, God laid it on my heart to write out a check and give it to you. I had just received some insurance money and had some extra to share. Just as I was walking out the door to come here, I got a phone call from a friend down-state. She needed me to come quickly, as someone we both knew was threatening suicide. I jumped straight in my car and took off, forgetting about your check.

As I was getting ready to leave down there, I got the flu and was sick in bed for days. I just got home and as I walked in the door God reminded me about the check and here I am. I am so sorry I couldn't get here last month."

Holding my breath I asked, "How much is the check?" The young man answered, "$50.00."

I did my usual "miracle-thing"...I screamed.

God is exciting as well as faithful.

Chapter 22
CHICKEN

Luke 22:35 And he said unto them, When I sent you without purse, and scrip, and shoes, lacked ye any thing? And they said, Nothing.

1 Corinthians 2:9 But as it is written, Eye hath not seen, nor ear heard, neither have entered into the heart of man, the things which God hath prepared for them that love him.

2 Corinthians 9:8 And God [is] able to make all grace abound toward you; that ye, always having all sufficiency in all [things], may abound to every good work:

Chicken was one of our favorite foods. Our taste-buds in this area were even compatible with the doctor's orders, "Eat lots of fat-free meat, like chicken"...we complied.

The day came when we were down to one little scrawny bird. Due to our fixed income, there was no hope of going to the store for more, and it was two weeks until payday. What were we to do?

Our pastor had said to go to God with ALL of our needs...even lack of chicken. So, Edward and I prayed. Then I remembered what Jesus said in Luke 6:38, "Give, and it shall be given unto you; good measure, pressed down, and shaken together, and running over, shall men give into your bosom. For with the same measure that ye mete withal it shall be measured to you again."

I said, "Edward, Love, we have two choices. We can either cut this puny chicken up in small pieces and stretch him out over the next two weeks for you, or we can ask someone to dinner to share it with...someone who can't pay us back. If we choose the latter then God will have to bless us one-hundred fold back. Then we will have more than enough to last until payday. Which will it be?"

Well, at this point, the good angel that sat on Edward's right shoulder, and the bad angel that sat on his left shoulder, got into a terrible fight, with Edward in the middle as arbitrator. Greed and selfishness struggled with faith in God to supply in time for tomorrow's dinner. Faith finally won out. We invited a divorced friend of Edward's and a widowed friend of mine to have dinner with us that evening.

As we were dinning with our guests, there was a knock on our door. One of the students from my art class was standing outside. When I asked her to come in she declined, saying, "I just need to talk to you privately." I stepped outside.

Let me stop here and insert some background infra-matron on this lady. My only contact with her was in the classes we were taking from the same art teacher. I knew nothing about her, where she lived, or even what she did for a living. We saw each other once a week and the most we said to one another was, "Hi" or, "Nice work."

In class, I always sat next to my dearest friend, and this lady sat in the adjoining room, but she could hear our conversations. My friend and I were constantly telling each other the latest miracle that Jesus had done for us. In fact, God was All we talked about. Now, here was this class-mate standing on my verandah, wanting to confide in me privately. Hummmmm...something was up.

After much hemming and hawing, looking embarrassed and clearing her throat, she said, "Lee, my husband and I raise beef cattle, and we just dressed out this year's supply for our family. We can't get it all into our freezer if we don't clean out last years leftovers. I don't want to insult you, or hurt your feelings, but would you and your husband like to have a bag of last year's ground beef?" At this point I did my usual miracle thing. I screamed!

When we got to her car, last years leftovers turned into twenty-five pounds of hamburger. When I saw this I said, "Whoa, this is MORE than enough to replace our puny little chicken... God is really up to something now."

Later that evening we got a call from a young man whom we had been teaching in the ways of God. He said, "Sister Lee, I want to get off of drugs, but I can't do it living at home. I need Christian influence. Would you and your husband let me stay with you until I get on my feet? "

To sum this all up, we traded a three pound chicken for twenty-five pounds of edible meat and God threw in a one hundred and forty pound pet-dear.

God is faithful and sneaky at the same time...in a good way of course.

Chapter 23
RAINBOW

Genesis 9:13 I do set my bow in the cloud, and it shall be for a token of a covenant between me and the earth.

Genesis 9:14 And it shall come to pass, when I bring a cloud over the earth, that the bow shall be seen in the cloud:

Genesis 9:16 And the bow shall be in the cloud; and I will look upon it, that I may remember the everlasting covenant between God and every living creature of all flesh that [is] upon the earth.

Edward and I, plus my daughter Lois, had cultivated some wonderful Christian friends. One couple, Fred and Betty, really stood out. Fred did auto-body work like Edward had, before he developed heart problems, and when Fred and Edward got together they could discuss cars for hours.

This couple loved to talk about Jesus and anytime someone was teaching the Bible they wanted to be there. Fred taught Sunday School at his church but he and his wife never missed Bible study at our house. In time, Betty became my partner as I traveled to various towns to teach. She would read the Bible to me as I drove to class and she and I would pray all the way home from class.

In the beginning of our friendship, Fred and Edward would start in on a discussion of Jesus after they had exhausted the subject of cars. As time went by, "The Boys", as we called them, began to start their conversations with Jesus and finally they didn't even discuss cars. Our faith levels in God's goodness were about the same.

One day while they were visiting with us it began to rain. We all ran for cover..."The Boys" to the garage and the girls to the house. Once in the house we-girls began to discuss different things we had read in the Bible. We got so happy over the ways of the Lord that we started praising and dancing around like teen-agers who are in love for the first time.

When we calmed down I looked outside. It had stopped raining and I said, "Look, you two. It has stopped raining and the weather conditions are just right for a rainbow. Let's ask God to send us one."

The girls agreed and we prayed for a rainbow...nothing else. As I was turning my head, and quicker than the bat of an eye, a double rainbow flashed across the sky. The under-bow was a normal, brightly colored rainbow. But the top one was so brilliant that we could hardly look at it. It was fully in sight from one end of the horizon to the other end.

It looked as if the sun was not causing this rainbow since one of its ends ended in the West where the sun was and the other was ending in the East. This left the arch facing us to the South.

People started coming out of their houses to look at it. Some stopped their cars to gaze at it. "The Boys" could hardly believe their eyes. We decided then and there that as Christians we short change ourselves. Does not the Bible say, "...you have not because you ask not"? (James 4:2)

God delights to give us the desires of our hearts.

Chapter 24
TRACTOR

Matthew 18:6 But whoso shall offend one of these little ones which believe in me, it were better for him that a millstone were hanged about his neck, and [that] he were drowned in the depth of the sea.

Mark 9:23 Jesus said unto him, If thou canst believe, all things [are] possible to him that believeth.

John 3:12 If I have told you earthly things, and ye believe not, how shall ye believe, if I tell you [of] heavenly things?

Edward had always wanted a full-size tractor. I had watched him gather parts from discarded machines of various sorts, put them together and build himself necessary equipment, like lawn mowers, snow blowers, and in time, a miniature bulldozer. Even though I admired his ability and resourcefulness, I knew that a full-size tractor was too involved to piece together...God would have to supply.

Fred, Edward's auto-body-repair friend, stopped by one day and casually mentioned that a man he worked for had bought a new tractor and now wanted to sell his old one. He was asking three hundred dollars for it. But there was a catch to it...the tractor wouldn't run. The fact that it wouldn't run didn't bother Edward a bit...he wanted to see it.

After viewing the tractor, Edward was convinced he could make it run, even though others had tried and failed. But no matter how hard Edward pressured, the farmer would not come down on his price. Edward came home without the tractor, but with a conviction that it was his.

By this time in our study of the Bible, Edward had finally realized that there was a difference between believing God's Word with one's head, and believing it with one's heart. Knowing this, if he wanted something that he thought might be in his head only, he would get me to join him in his prayer request. Edward really believed that God would give me anything that I asked Him for.

Even though at times I wanted to trade Edward for a one way ticket out of Michigan, he knew that in my heart he was the apple-of-my-eye, just as we are the apple-of-God's-eye. I joined with him in faith and asked God for the money to buy the tractor.

During this time as I went to teach my Bible classes in the surrounding towns, Edward would drive me. One of my students, who lived in Charlevoix, Michigan, owned her own business, and had been acting like she had something on her mind for the previous two weeks... but just couldn't bring herself to express it. Even Edward had noticed it.

At the next class in her town, I asked everyone to join their faith with ours in our request for Edward's tractor. After class, the business owner came up to me and said, "Here is some money. God has been dealing with me for two weeks to give this mad-money to you, and I just couldn't bring myself to part with it. You see, I keep some money back from my business. Then, when I get mad at my husband, I go on a buying spree. God has been showing me in this class that I shouldn't do this.

The lady had the money clenched up tightly in her fist. I never saw it as it touched my hand...but, two one-hundred dollar bills flashed across my mind and I gasped. On the way home, I took the money out to count it. There was exactly two one-hundred dollar bills. But, the tractor was three hundred dollars. Here was a mystery.

The next day I said to Edward, "Why don't you go over and offer the man two-hundred dollars cash. If this is the Lord's work he will take it." While he was making plans to go, Fred called and said, "I talked to the farmer again and he decided that he will take two hundred cash for his tractor."

Fred towed the tractor home behind his truck, while Edward sat up on the seat guiding it. They made all of ten miles an hour with Edward grinning and waving to everyone the whole way.

Once it was on top of our hill, someone suggested that Edward try turning the engine over with the key one more time...he did. That tractor started right up without even a sputter and purred like a kitten. The five of us onlookers and Edward had a screaming "Hallelujah Party" right there on top of that hill.

God had shown Himself strong in our behalf, again.

Chapter 25
STRAWBERRIES

Job 40:4 Behold, I am vile; what shall I answer thee? I will lay mine hand upon my mouth.

Psalms 38:4 For mine iniquities are gone over mine head: as an heavy burden they are too heavy for me.

Psalms 38:18 For I will declare mine iniquity; I will be sorry for my sin.

A year before we got The tractor, someone gave me two rows of rare and expensive strawberry plants. Edward advised me to plant them in the middle of our garden so the man who did our plowing wouldn't plow them under...I did.

The next year, God presented Edward with his own full size tractor. Now he could plow up his own garden and play at farming all he wanted to.

He had been plowing for about an hour when I heard him come into the house, plop down on the couch and let out a long deep sigh. This usually spelled trouble.

"What is wrong, Sweetheart?" I asked. "I buried my tractor up to the hub caps," he replied. We lived close to a lake and the soil was very sandy in spots...apparently he had found one of the spots. I looked out the window and there sat his tractor buried just as he said.

Wanting to see how much he had finished before disaster struck, I glanced around the whole garden. He had done a fine job. There wasn't a weed, nor unplowed spot in the whole front yard...nor were there any strawberry plants.

Turning to look at him I said, "Love, where are my strawberry plants?"

"I plowed them under," he said. "You what?" I asked incredulously. "I plowed them under."

"Why?" I yelled in shock and disbelief. "It was too much trouble to turn the tractor around each time, he replied."

"Why didn't you call me so I could move them?" I whined. "I didn't want to get off the tractor," he answered.

"Edward, you yourself told me to put them there so they would be safe. This was their second year and they were ready to produce for us." I was so heartbroken and angry I didn't trust myself to say another word, so I hurried to my bedroom, threw myself on the bed and cried. Them I began to dialogue with the "Almighty."

Sitting and looking upward I said, "Father God, do you see what that son of yours did out there. He plowed my strawberries under. He didn't even TRY to save them. That is not fair. What am I going to do?"

Fully expecting God to answer, He didn't let me down. "Forgive him," God said.

In shocked disbelief I said, "What did You say?" Again from deep inside me I heard, "Forgive him for running over your strawberries."

"No way, Father God, he is not even sorry he did it." Quicker than lighting, God shot back with, "Neither were you when I sent My Son down on earth to pay for your sins and give you forgiveness."

Feeling real shame inside me, I ducked my head, raised my eyeballs and said, "Gosh God, You sure do know how to hurt a person."

So, off I went to do my duty. We had a very large living room that held two couches and Edward had moved from the one beside the front door to the one nearest the hall where I was. As I came around the hall door there he was laying very peacefully on the couch as if nothing had happened. He didn't even look sad.

I looked down at him and said, "Edward, I forgive you for running over my strawberry plants. I know that you didn't mean to."

Not opening his eyes and in a monotone voice he said, "Yes I did."

God had been dealing with me about the anger that would raise up inside me when I was confronted with resistance from anything or anybody. Now, here was open-resistance laying on MY couch. (The other couch was his.) I felt a twinge of anger churn in my stomach. Then I heard the Lord whisper, "Stop." Not realizing that hardheadedness goes along with anger, I said, "No Lord, I got it together. I'm not going to loose it."

To Edward I said, "No, Love, I know that deep inside you, you really didn't mean to do it." This time he opened one eye, put a smirky grin on his face, and in a very nasty tone said, "Yes I did."

Well now, this forgiveness business was turning out to be harder than I had anticipated. Once again, I felt anger surge inside my stomach. It wanted to blast that "Little Frenchman" with a few red-hot flames of choice names like you "Dumb Idiot" or "Lame Brain Moron"...but I suppressed it. Inside me, I could barely hear the faint whisper of God's Spirit again saying, "Stop!"

Knowing I had changed from the old-me to the self-confident, completely-in-control Lee, I said, "No, Father God, I am all right. I told You, I got it together."

So, looking down at Edward I said, "Sweetheart, I don't care what you say. I know you. And I know that deep down inside you really are a nice guy and you really didn't mean to run over my strawberries, you dumb *#%@^%&*. (Yes, it was a dirty four letter word.)

Now let me say this in my defense. I really didn't mean to call him a dirty name. Nor did I even THINK a dirty name. I had given all this up with the penny jar. To tell you the truth I don't know WHERE that word sprang up from. It just slipped out as if it were greased and was the attached-caboose of the word Dumb.

Just as soon as I said it, I turned around, and slowly headed back to the conference room for another conversation with the "BOSS". Humiliation hung on me like a heavy, rain-soaked, woolen shroud.

Tears rolled down my face as I looked up and meekly said, "Well Father God, I'm back. I blew it. I am rotten to the core. Please forgive me and take all this ugliness out of me, and make me "Christ" like...and what do I do now?"

God's next words blew me away. He said, "Well, now you have to ask him to forgive you for calling him a dirty name and then you have to forgive him for running over the straw-berries."

I could hardly believe my ears. My tears dried up and in a shocked tone I said, "Wow, no wonder so many left You. These teachings are too hard." (John 6:60, 66)

As I sat there meditating on the soon-to-come scene, I reverted back to my childhood days of shrewdness. I said, "Uhhhh, Father God, what are the consequences if I don't ask forgiveness?" He said, "You know how bad you feel inside right now? Well, you will stay like that until you straighten this out."

As I sat there and pondered over the things God had said I realized what the Bible, in Genesis, Chapter Three, had been trying to teach me. Just like Adam and Eve had broken fellowship with God by sin, I had done the same thing.

Fellowship with God brings the "Joy" of the Holy Spirit to us. Sin, or to rephrase the word sin, "acting-ungodly", grieves the Holy Spirit inside us. When He is grieved His Joy shuts down. Without His Joy in us this world becomes ugggggly.

This Joylessness was the way I had felt for years before I really understood the relationship with the living Jesus Christ. I made a quick, quality decision. I did not want to go back to depression, sadness and feeling lonely. If asking Edward to forgive me for calling him a dirty word was all it took to get the "Joy" back, then lead this lamb to the slaughter-room.

Edward was a very forgiving man...I became a forgiving woman.

By the way, God dealt with Edward months later to bring about his repentance over the strawberries.

God is a God of fairness.

Chapter 26
SLOW DOWN

Psalms 37:4 Delight thyself also in the LORD; and he shall give thee the desires of thine heart.

Edward had loved deer hunting since he was a young boy. By the time I met him he had turned into a great deer-poacher. He would ride around at night spotting deer with a light from his car. The deer would freeze in the light while Edward would pick them off. He never missed a shot and he always got his quota for the season. In fact he was notorious for his excellent marksmanship. To give him some credit, he never killed just for the fun of killing. It was a matter of really needing the meat for the dinner table.

Then Jesus came into his life. Edward's conscience began to function and with much, much, sadness he hung up his spotting light. He went legitimate. All of a sudden his quota dropped. It seems a deer in the daytime is much harder to kill than one under the powerful beam of a spotlight.

Now instead of the joyful, excited man I married, I was living with a sad, depressed, woe-is-me stranger. Neither I nor any of his friends could cheer him up. He felt like God was punishing him for all his past deer seasons of forbidden-fruit harvests.

I tried to get him to practice his shooting...this held no interest for him. Then each day of hunting grew shorter and shorter and finally he began to loose his desire to even go hunting with his friends. His deer stories began to dry-up...he was silently grieving.

He and I began to ride around at dusk watching the deer come out of hiding to graze. Edward could spot a deer in the edge of the woods three football fields away while driving fifty miles an hour. He began to tell his friends and me about the lovely, graceful deer he spotted while driving alone. God was slowly changing Edward's outlook on deer.

The hunting season finally arrived when Edward couldn't shoot any more deer. He came home all excited and happy telling me about his experience. "Dear, you should have been there. I heard this snap over to the left, and I raised my gun."

"Yes, yes." I said.

"I was ready to blow him away as soon as he walked into my sights. I released the safety on my gun and had my finger in a squeezed position."

"YES, YES, EDWARD. AND THEN WHAT HAPPENED?" I asked in my excitement.

"Dear, the most beautiful buck you ever saw stepped out right in front of me. It was the really old one that we have been chasing for years... and he was standing right in my line of fire."

"EDWARD, JUST TELL ME WHAT HAPPENED!" I yelled.

"I couldn't shoot him," he answered.

"WHY?" I countered.

"He was just so beautiful I couldn't do it. I didn't have the heart. He has escaped all of us for so long, it just didn't seem right."

Edward was his old self again. He was smiling his secretive little smile like he had his own private joke going, just as he use to do when he had been sneaking illegal deer. God and Edward were on good terms again.

The winter that year just got colder and colder and snow piled up everywhere. The deer began to come out in the broad daylight to forge for food. Everyone talked about how bad it was for the little critters and the deer.

One morning Edward was driving to Gaylord, Michigan, which was about a half an hour away from us. As he was traveling down the highway he distinctively heard the Lord say, "Slow down."

Edward looked down at his speedometer and saw that he was going five miles over the speed limit so he cut back five. Again he heard the Lord tell him, "Slow down."

This time he began to argue with God. "Look, God, I did what You said. I cut my speed back. I'm going the legal speed limit. Once more God said, "Slow down."

"Ok, I'm doing it. But I don't see why You.....WOW."

Before Edward could finish his sentence, a whole herd of deer came charging out of the nearby trees and jumped over the roadway.

As Edward told about this encounter with the Lord and the deer, his eyes were as big as silver dollars. He said, "Dear, if I had not obeyed God the first time I would have missed the whole scene. If I had not obeyed Him the second time, they would have landed on the top of my car and I would be history. There were at least twenty five deer in that herd. God is really something..."

Well, between you and me, twenty five deer sounded like a lot of deer to me, but one thing is for sure..God is faithful. He says in Psalms 37:4, "Delight thyself also in the Lord; and He shall give thee the desires of thine heart." God most certainly met one of Edward's desires that day.

Chapter 27
COWS

Genesis 1:26 And God said, Let us make man in our image, after our likeness: and let them have dominion over the fish of the sea, and over the fowl of the air, and over the cattle, and over all the earth, and over every creeping thing that creepeth upon the earth.

Psalms 8:6 Thou madest him to have dominion over the works of thy hands; thou hast put all [things] under his feet:

Psalms 72:8 He shall have dominion also from sea to sea, and from the river unto the ends of the earth.

My pastor had just given me a college level course on Demonology to study. I did not like the course nor could I see any use for it. In fact, it rather frightened me at times but I was laboring through it.

My husband and I lived in a house that was sitting on a hill and the only level place was the front yard. We had planted a garden the same year I was given the college course and the produce of the garden was growing well.

One morning I was on the phone talking about Jesus to my dearest friend. I was working in my kitchen at the time and on one of my turns I glanced out the window. To my surprise the garden was full of white-faced cows having breakfast in our corn and beans.

I told my friend I would have to go down and chase the cows out of the garden. When I said this, I heard a whisper from inside me say, "No, do it from here." Then I remembered what I had just studied in the Demonology course about the Christian having the authority over the enemy. This was certainly the enemy influencing these cows.

But I also remembered the verse in Genesis 1:26 that says mankind has authority over the birds, fish, cattle, creeping things and over all the earth. And Pastor had said that even though

Adam sold out to the enemy in this area, when we accept Jesus we get that authority back.

Courage rose up inside me. Strength and determination took over. I said to my friend, "Hey, I don't have to go down there. I can command them to leave from up here. The Bible says I have the authority, isn't that right?"

With the phone still at my ear, I pointed to the cows with my fore-finger and yelled down at them from my window, "Cows, you get out of my garden." Well those animals didn't even stop to take a breather...they just kept munching. Then I added, "In the name of Jesus!"

When I said Jesus, twelve white faces whirled upward to glare at me in the window. It was such a shock to see that many cows swing their heads all at one time that the bravery I possessed left me instantly and I instinctively stepped backward in my own kitchen. There I was two stories up with a brick wall and three-hundred yards between them and me and I was turning into a sniveling coward.

As quick as the fear hit, my spirit said, "You can't quit now. You will never know if it works or not." So, fortified with follow-through, I once more stepped to the window.

I said, "Cows, you heard me. You go home right now." At this point I thought of the traffic on the road. I didn't want the cows to get hit rushing pell-mell down the road. So, I said, "You go down my driveway, across the road, up the road to your driveway, straight up your driveway and into your barn."

And like before, I could have been the wind whistling through the trees for all they cared. Until I said, "In the name of Jesus."

At the name of Jesus, those cows whirled around, threw their tails in the air, raced down my driveway, crossed the road, rushed up the side of the highway, took a sharp left into their driveway and dashed in their barn pushing and shoving each other the whole way.

I was watching all this from the safety of my window and telling my friend, "You are not going to believe this! No...Yes,

You would! Oh, how exciting! They are doing it! They are doing just what I told them to do! Isn't God great!"

There was a time when God sent me to a ranch down in the wilds of Mexico and some dogs wanted to have me for lunch. Having this experience behind me helped save me from early extinction.

God is our protection.

Chapter 28
WINDOW

Psalms 31:2 Bow down thine ear to me; deliver me speedily: be thou my strong rock, for an house of defence to save me.

Psalms 37:40 And the LORD shall help them, and deliver them: he shall deliver them from the wicked, and save them, because they trust in him.

Psalms 55:16 As for me, I will call upon God; and the LORD shall save me.

We had prayed for a garage and God had blessed us with an old, one room school house. The only price requirement was hauling it from the original site to our house...about a mile. We were powerless to arrange the move.

Meeting our neighbor at the mail box, Edward casually mentioned the loss of our chance to have a garage. Our neighbor was a Deputy Sheriff plus a farmer. He understood the importance of a garage in upper Michigan.

He also knew of Edward's heart condition and liked the gutsy little Frenchman. (He had insisted that we call him, day or night, if Edward began having trouble with his heart.)

The Deputy organized the neighbors around us and arranged the whole trip. Bringing tractors, flat beds, flag men, etc., they maneuvered it down the road and up the hill to our house. It was quite a sight to see.

Once it was settled in place Edward began to renovate it to suit his purposes. The final touch was a metal storm door on the north side of the building that became the main doorway for people.

This door had two glass panels in it and each time we went in or out the glass panels would rattle. The door also had a mind of its own. No matter what we did to it, the wind would catch it and slam it either against the garage or its own frame.

Edward's famous command to me as I entered the garage was, "Watch the door. Don't let it break." Going out of the garage I heard the same thing.

Now this wouldn't have been so bad if I only went in and out once or twice a week. But sometimes I would help him paint a car for someone and I would make ten or twelve trips in and out that door in a day's time.

I tried everything I knew, short of a temper fit, to convince him I would be careful with his door. Oh yes, the garage had now stopped being OUR garage and had turned into HIS garage and HIS door. I finally told on him to Father God. I prayed that God would deal with Edward about the door.

One day, shortly after I prayed, Edward came dragging into the house like he had lost his best friend. In a flash I knew what had happened. "You broke the glass in your door, didn't you...," I stated rather than asked.

"The wind ripped it right out of my hand. It broke the new chain holding it, and smashed into a million pieces against the wall," he whined.

"Wow," I said, "I'm sure glad it was you and not me that broke it. If it was me you would never have forgiven me."

"You are right," he said.

"Love," I said excitedly, "This is just like we are learning in church...you were snared by the words of your mouth. You spoke it every time someone went in or out. Fear of it breaking clouded out the blessing. Or to put it another way, "The things I feared, have come upon me." (Job 3:25)."

We prayed and God blessed Edward with another door panel. From then on it was safe for everyone to go in and out without the usual command of, "Don't break the door." He never mentioned it again, nor did the door ever break again.

God's ways are higher than our ways...

Chapter 29
HEART ATTACK

Matthew 8:16 When the even was come, they brought unto him many that were possessed with devils: and he cast out the spirits with [his] word, and healed all that were sick:

Matthew 9:6 But that ye may know that the Son of man hath power on earth to forgive sins, (then saith he to the sick of the palsy) Arise, take up thy bed, and go unto thine house.

James 5:14 Is any sick among you? let him call for the elders of the church; and let them pray over him, anointing him with oil in the name of the Lord:

James 5:15 And the prayer of faith shall save the sick, and the Lord shall raise him up; and if he have committed sins, they shall be forgiven him.

Edward had a heart valve replacement years before we married. Shortly after we married the Doctors told us he needed another one but his health was too bad to risk it. We lived with the constant threat that his heart could quit any minute.

Several years after we were married, the Lord worked another of His famous miracles and Edward was blessed with free lumber to build an addition to our garage. Edward was a hard worker even with his sick heart. But this was a bigger job then Edward had anticipated and winter was coming-on fast...he began to push himself to get done. He started to look bad, his appetite dropped off and he became grumpy. When he sat down to rest he dozed off to sleep within minutes. Then the day came that I heard him scream at me from his building project, "Lee, bring me a drink of water, NOW!" Edward always called me "Dear," not Lee and he NEVER ordered me around...something was wrong.

Running to the garage with his water, I began praying. As I entered Edward was sitting in his usual resting-chair, white as a sheet. My old, full length lounge chair was next to his chair, so I offered to swing him around to it so he could lie down.

I had worked in nursing homes and knew the procedure for transferring patients from a chair to a bed, without dropping them or breaking my back. As I swung him he went dead weight in my arms. When I had him secured on the edge of the lounge and began to lay him down, he started to froth at the mouth and make the gurgling sounds of death. Edward was dying in my arms. My mind said, "Call an ambulance."

We lived seven miles from town and it was thirty miles to the nearest hospital. God was the only one who could help us. So, grabbing Edward up close to my bosom, I yelled at God, "Father God, tell me what to do! Tell me what to do, RIGHT NOW!" I cocked my head sideways like I always do when I am really intent on hearing something...I heard nothing.

All this time my mind was going ballistics on me saying, "Put him down and get an ambulance fast. He is dying and it will be your fault!"

But, as I tried once more to lay him down, he started to gurgle again, only now the froth was bubbling out like someone had poured washing powder inside him.

I again screamed at God, and this time I even shook my fist at Him, "God didn't You hear me? This is Your baby, Lee! You said in Your word that I am the apple-of-Your-eye. Well, Edward is the apple-of-my-eye. I want him to live. Tell me what to do, and tell me RIGHT NOW!" Again I cocked my ear to listen for His answer. This time I heard a whisper from deep inside my being. It was very clear and strong like a command. It said, "Take charge!"

Our Pastor had taken a "Demonology" course in College and had encouraged me to study it. After reading several pages I would get so depressed that I would lay it aside determined to forget the whole thing. To motivate me to study again, God would arrange to send me someone that needed what I had not studied. Feeling guilty that I could not help them, I would once more pick up the book and go-at-it. Thank God, I had just completed the course and knew what "Take charge" meant.

I had learned that Jesus says in Luke 9:1, ".... that we have the authority over ALL devils...." They CAN NOT do anything to us that we don't allow. I learned in Psalms 90:10, that "The days of our years are threescore years and ten....." This is a minimum of seventy years of life that God has given to us, if we choose to fight for it.

Then in John 10:10, I learned, "The thief cometh not, but for to steal, and to kill, and to destroy...." And in 2 Corinthians 10:4, "For the weapons of our warfare are not carnal, but mighty through God to the pulling down of strong holds;..."

Ephesians 6:12 told me, "For we wrestle not against flesh and blood, but against principalities, against powers, against the rulers of the darkness of this world, against spiritual wickedness in high places." And last, it says in Ephesians 6:17, "And take the helmet of salvation, and the sword of the Spirit, which is the word of God." I understood what the "Whisper" was telling me...I needed to get busy.

I turned (still holding Edward in my arms) to the side of me, and looking up a little, I shook my fist and said, "I bind you Satan, in the name Jesus. Get your hands off Edward. I bind you, spirit of death. God said we have seventy years to live so you can't have Edward."

At this point I could no longer ignore what my mind was saying. I threw Edward down and ran for the phone. On the way out of the garage I looked back and said, "Edward is Your problem God, my job is to call an ambulance."

When I returned to the garage Edward was still on the lounge but he was awake and sounded drunker-than-a-skunk. When I questioned him he said, "Issssss feeeeeel fineeeee." He was so full of the Power of God he couldn't see or talk straight.

When the ambulance arrived, the paramedics were so sure Edward would not survive, that they put D.O.A on his chart...dead on arrival. But by the time I got to the hospital Edward was sitting up on the examining table, entertaining the nurses. The doctor was trying to listen to his chest and puzzlement was written all over his face.

He said, "I can't understand it. This man has had congestive heart failure, but I can't find any fluid in his lungs. They should be full." Then he pointed to the x-ray of Edward's heart saying, "Look at all these spots. This is the times that his heart stopped. He died that many times, but there is no sign of any fluid now. I don't know what happened to it."

I said, "Are you a Christian?" "Yes," he replied.

"Then let me tell you what happened."

With that, I began to explain the scenario of the spirit of death verses the Spirit of God, and that God had obviously won....

Chapter 30
INSULIN

1 Corinthians 12:8 For to one is given by the Spirit the word of wisdom; to another the word of knowledge by the same Spirit;

2 Corinthians 10:5 Casting down imaginations, and every high thing that exalteth itself against the knowledge of God, and bringing into captivity every thought to the obedience of Christ;

Colossians 1:9 For this cause we also, since the day we heard [it], do not cease to pray for you, and to desire that ye might be filled with the knowledge of his will in all wisdom and spiritual understanding;

After Edward's heart attack, the doctors wanted to keep him in the hospital under observation for three days. So off to the intensive care unit he went. The nursing staff told us, "Only one person can visit with him at a time and then only for ten minutes every hour." These orders seemed simple enough to follow.

On Saturday nights Edward and I hung out with a group of ministers from various churches who had music practice sessions at Brother Bud's house. Bud, like me, had been raised in Kentucky, and loved the Lord. He and a fellow minister played guitars. Edward would bring his guitar and once in a while we were blessed with a banjo picking Pharmacist.

Most of the remaining adults joined in with singing, stopping now and then so Bud and his wife could practice some of their duets. Kids ran in and out, playing and pouting. The phone would ring off the hook and some mothers would begin discussions about anything from soup, to the President of the United States.

By the end of the night, we had consumed all the food that was supplied by Bud and his wife and gathered at the kitchen table to pray and swap stories of the miracles that the Lord had created for us. This was not church. This was fun, relaxation and a group of neighbors bonded together by the love of Jesus.

When the musicians found out Edward was in the hospital, they rushed over to pray for him...all except Bud. When he called I felt that the Lord said that he was not to come now.

There were so many guys in the hall of the intensive care unit, and remembering what the nurse had instructed us about people and time limits, I was afraid they would throw us all out! I finally prayed, "Lord, You said in John 14:14 that if we ask ANYTHING in Your name, You will do it. Well, please blind the eyes of the nurses so they won't see but one person and let one hour be as ten minutes to them."

From then, to late that night, Edward's room was full of praying, joking preacher/musicians cheering us up and not one complaint was heard from the nursing staff.

Months later I went to Bible School with Carol, one of the nurses who was on duty that night. When I tried to tell the class how many of us were in that hospital room and for how long of a time, Carol wouldn't believe me. She said, "No, I was there. I know there was only one person at a time and for only ten minutes every hour. And YOU sure didn't stay in there all night. I would have had you thrown out." Hummmm....seems like I remember telling SOMEONE that very same thing.

Everyone finally left Edward's room that night and peace descended on the "Intensive Care Unit" of the hospital. Sometime in the early a.m. the nurse came running into Edward's room. She began checking machines and looking worried. When I inquired what was wrong, she said, "His blood pressure is taking a nose dive and I can't figure out why." As she ran out the door to call the doctor the Lord spoke to my heart and said, "It is now time to call Brother Bud for prayer support."

I told the nurse I was going to a phone down the hall and I would be right back. On my way back from calling Bud, I was talking to God. "Lord, in 1 Corinthians 12 You said that there are nine gifts for the church today, and the Word of Knowledge is one of them. I am one of Your church and I need that gift right now. The nurses and doctors don't know what is wrong with Edward and he could die if You don't do something for us and do it fast."

The word insulin flashed in my mind. I said, "Lord, what has insulin got to do with Edward's situation?" He brought to my memory that the doctors had given Edward a shot of insulin when he came into the hospital around seven p.m. His blood sugar was sky high due to the heart episode. Edward had not been on insulin for a while, nor had he eaten anything since breakfast... he was having an insulin attack.

Hurrying up, I could hardly wait to tell the nurse. Then I stopped dead in my tracts. Looking up at God, I said, "Whoa here God... just a minute. If I go in there and tell that nurse that YOU told me it is an insulin attack, she will call the little men in the white coats and have me committed...no way am I going to do this!"

Then I remembered something else. "Hey God, it also says in Chapter 12 verse 8, that the Word of Wisdom is another one of those nine gifts. I need that gift too, so I will have the wisdom to make that nurse think she is the one who figured all this out."

As I hurried up to the desk I could see that the nurse was frantic. No one knew what was happening to Edward, so nonchalantly, I began to talk about Edward, his heart, insulin, eating and sugar. I don't even remember what I said or how I said it, except that I was just making small talk.

All of a sudden the nurse jumped up and yelled, "Insulin! He could be having an insulin attack. Quick, let's get some orange juice down him." The orange juice saved the day and Edward. Shortly thereafter Bud came through the door and joined with me in bathing Edward with prayer. From then on he did fine and was released three days later.

It is amazing what God will do for us....if we can only believe what His "INSTRUCTION Book" says.

Chapter 31
WOODS

Psalms 4:8 I will both lay me down in peace, and sleep: for thou, LORD, only makest me dwell in safety.

Psalms 127:2 [It is] vain for you to rise up early, to sit up late, to eat the bread of sorrows: [for] so he giveth his beloved sleep.

Proverbs 3:24 When thou liest down, thou shalt not be afraid: yea, thou shalt lie down, and thy sleep shall be sweet.

After Edward was released from the hospital, a friend gave us some money to take a week-end vacation and relax. We felt that the Lord wanted us to go camping, so we prayed for God to show us just the right place. It was a pure faith trip. We headed North and stopped wherever and whenever we felt the Lord wanted us to stop.

At one of our stops, as we visited with other travelers, we found we were at the turn-point on the highway to go to the camp grounds of the great North Woods in upper Michigan. We headed there.

We had fixed up the back of Edward's truck with a mattress and had packed our cooking utensils along the sides. The only thing we had forgotten was our mosquito repellent.

When we found just the right spot near a lake we bunched rocks together to cook on. After strolling around the lake we settled in to sleep under the stars. It was CLOSE to heaven on earth.

The following year, about the same time, we decided to go back to the woods and have another wonderful weekend. Only this time we failed to ask the Lord what He wanted us to do. We just took it for granted it was ok for us to go to the same place.

For this trip some friends of ours had loaned us their pop-up camper to pull behind our truck. No more dew falling in our faces, no more mosquitoes biting, nor rock gathering... we were to be big-time campers!

Half way there it started to rain. Edward had to drive slower than we planned due to pulling the trailer and the slick road. It wasn't just dark when we got there, it was pitch black.

We weren't too sure about the condition of the road when it was wet, so we decided to camp for the night at the first clearing we came to. When daylight came we would take inventory, and if it looked safe, we would amble on down to the lake.

When morning came it was still raining. We hung around inside the camper praying for it to stop. About noon, there was a break in the clouds so we decided to walk down to the lake and check out the road on the way.

As we walked along, we heard voices coming from back in the woods. Glancing around we were shocked to see motorcycles parked everywhere, with rough, tough, tattooed men covered in pictures from their ears to their ankle bones staring at us.

Edward said, "We are in big trouble." It started to rain again and by the time we ran back to our camper it was pouring. We decided to wait until the rain slacked off to pack up the camper and head out of there.

Evening settled in and it was still pouring down rain. It was so dark by the time it did quit raining that we knew we would have to spend the night...we couldn't see to fold up the camper.

As we prepared to turn in for the night, we heard an explosion of motorcycle engines start up. As some of them came past our camper, they stopped and started asking me what seemed to be harmless questions.

"Don't answer them. Those questions are loaded. No matter what you answer you are going to get a dirty statement back," Edward said.

How do you know that?" I asked. "I was in a motorcycle gang for a while. I know what I'm talking about. Just don't say anything," he replied. Edward looked so worried I tried to cheer him up. I said, "It is ok, Love, they are leaving." He said, "No, Dear, they are just going to town to get drunk. When the bars close they will be back and longing for trouble. They will be looking for us."

I said, "Oh Edward, let's pray. God will take care of us. He says in His Word that He gives His angels charge over us. And that no hurt or harm can come to us. He also says He gives His beloved sweet sleep." I grabbed his hand and prayed.

The next morning Edward got up late. He looked like he had gone from bags-to-suitcases under his eyes. I said, "Love, what is wrong. Is your heart hurting?" "I didn't get any sleep," he said. "Why?" I asked. "Didn't you hear them?" he asked.

"Hear who?" I asked.

"The motorcycle gang."

"Did they come back?" I asked.

"You mean you didn't hear them?" he asked incredulously. "There were about a dozen of them circling this camper shouting drunken obscenities. They wanted you and were close enough to rip this canvas top with their knives. And I didn't have a gun or even a knife." Now MY eyes were as big as saucers. "Love, I didn't hear a thing after we prayed and went to sleep."

Once more God had fulfilled His Word. He HAD given His beloved "sweet sleep." He is SO faithful....

Chapter 32
TRIP

Mark 4:40 And he said unto them, Why are ye so fearful? how is it that ye have no faith?

Mark 11:22 And Jesus answering saith unto them, Have faith in God.

Luke 17:19 And he said unto him, Arise, go thy way: thy faith hath made thee whole.

The day came that Edward and I finally believed what we were told in Psalms 37:4, "..........God will give us the desires of our heart." This seemed too good to be true, but like everything else we were learning, we decided to check this out to see if it REALLY was true.

As we discussed some of the desires-of-our-hearts Edward said, "I would love to go to Florida. I've heard so much about it and most of my friends have gone there...but I never have."

The following spring, Edward received some extra money and decided to take us to Kentucky to visit my Father. While we were preparing to go, Psalms 37:4 kept running through my mind. As I figured the expenses to Kentucky, I was overwhelmed with the thought that we were going on to Florida, and to figure that in also...and I was to tell no-one the amount.

The morning we were to leave I said, "We are going on to Florida after we stop at my Dad's house." When he and my daughter got over the shock of the announcement, Edward asked where the money was coming from for such a trip. I smiled and said, "God will supply. Did He not say in His Bible that He would give us the desires of our heart?" Now, inwardly I had NO idea where God would come up with this amount of money, but I never voiced my thoughts to anyone."

When we got to my Father's house, the first thing he wanted to do was plan our week's stay with him. I said, "Daddy, we are only here for two days. We are going on to Florida." At this statement, my Father sat very still, looking off into the distance for what seemed like ten minutes. Finally, he looked around at me and said, "Then you will need some spending money." Except for ten dollars less, he wrote me out a check for the exact amount that I had figured the cost of the trip to be. The ten dollars less puzzled me, but I told no one. This generosity to fund our spending money for a vacation trip was unlike my father. He was MORE than helpful if someone had a need but not for a frivolous thing like a fun trip. He had only taken mother and me on one vacation in our entire lives.

I also had not shared with my father our financial lack and our trust in God to fund the trip.

We went on to Florida, stayed a week, and headed back home to Michigan. As we filled up at the final service center we would have to stop in, I gave the man our last ten dollars for gas. Suddenly, I understood why my father gave me ten dollars less than I had budgeted.

When I added up the mileage for our trip, I had calculated for the swing over in Kentucky...from the interstate to my Father's place. On the way home we came straight through on the interstate and the mileage was exactly ten dollars less in gasoline.

God is a much better planner than I am, and He does give us the desires of our heart.

Chapter 33
SAWDUST

Matthew 21:22 And all things, whatsoever ye shall ask in prayer, believing, ye shall receive.

Romans 12:12 Rejoicing in hope; patient in tribulation; continuing instant in prayer;

Philippians 4:6 Be careful for nothing; but in every thing by prayer and supplication with thanksgiving let your requests be made known unto God.

After the miraculous healing the Lord had performed on me in 1980, my muscles were very weak from lack of use. It would take years before they were built up enough to endure hard work over an extended period of time so until then, I had to be careful and enlist the help of others on any large projects.

The summer after my healing we were blessed again with strawberry plants...a thousand of them. Our soil was so sandy we were told to lace it with mulch to hold water. After checking our finances we agreed it would have to be something free...so we prayed. Many phone calls and questions later, we were told sawdust would make good mulch and that there was a large hill of it free-for-the-taking. The Railroad had brought the sawdust in years ago but didn't need it all, so they had opened it up to the public...and I was a "Public."

Loading up our truck with a large assortment of tools with which to work, my daughter Lois and I set off together to glean the answer to our prayers. On the way, Lois remembered an appointment she had. "Mom, I don't know how long I'll be there, so maybe we should wait until tomorrow to get the sawdust. I don't want you out there digging and maybe hurting yourself." I agreed and dropped her off at her destination.

On my way home, I was singing and praising God as usual. When I arrived at the turn-off to our road, I just couldn't turn the wheel. It was like God was saying, "Do it yourself." So, armed with God's approval, I went to the mountain of sawdust. It was around two or three stories high and hard as a rock on the surface. Once the outer crust was broken open the sawdust was soft and easy to dig. I just had to cut through the crust. That couldn't be too hard of a job.

My first attempt was a wash-out. I was trying to dig too high up on the hill. I couldn't even make a scratch in it. Next to the base of the pile I found just the right spot. I set the blade of my shovel on it and jumped on the shovel with both my feet to get plenty of pressure on the cut. You guessed it. My muscles didn't hold. Both of my feet slipped off and I landed face down in the hill. I looked around to see if anyone was watching me. I was so embarrassed. Three or four more attempts like this left me breathless, sweating, and dirty as a coal miner. I said, "Ok God, I guess I'm not using the right tool." Going back to the truck, I grabbed up a nice heavy pick ax. I said, "All right God. This should do it." Raising the ax above my head to get more power when it fell into the crust, it tried to come crashing down on my head. Once more the lack of muscles had overpowered the situation. Clearly, I was not cut out for this line of work. Still, I had not exhausted all my resources yet...so back to the truck I went and gathered up all the implements we had brought. "Ok God, now let's get this job done, quickly."

Thinking I could just scrape the top off, I tried using the leaf rake and broke off a couple of its teeth. The regular rake wasn't any better. I slammed it down with a double handed, over the head "Karate-Chop" which glued the rake into the crust and I had to dig each little tooth out by hand. Now, before you condemn me as that-dumb-woman let it be said in my behalf, "I do try." Not having any better success with the rest of the tools I sat down on the back of our truck, and let God have it! "Father God, this was your idea and you were supposed to help me. Nothing I've tried so far has worked. You could have sent me angels to help, but did You? Oh no, You just sit up there watching me sweat and strain getting nowhere"...I quietly cried.

Then I remembered Matthew 17:20 in the Bible. I said, "Lord You said that if I had faith as a grain of a mustard seed, I could say to this mountain to move from here to there and it would have to obey me. Did You not say that? Those WERE Your Words, weren't they? Well, I command that mountain to fill up my truck." God began giving me thoughts, "Look at that hill." I saw that people had dug at the bottom of the hill and caused a cavern to form at the base. About head-high to me, a large overhang had formed. "Back your truck into that cavern and bump the back wall," He said. Yes! Yes! I could see it. He was going to make it fall into my truck. Great! Jumping into the truck I began backing. But when I got close to the back wall I slowed down and barely touched the sawdust. This time I heard, "Back up and bump the wall hard." Well now, God didn't have Edward for a husband.

I said, "Look God, if I do that I might break a tail light or dent the fender. Either way Edward will kill me. Couldn't we just nudge it hard?" Again I heard, "Back up and bump the wall hard." Well, it has been my experience that God only tells me the same thing three times and if I don't cooperate by the third time... He quits.

"Ok God, I am going to do this Your way...but if I hurt this truck I am going to tell Edward it was all Your fault. You told me to do it." Giving it the gas, I rammed the truck into that sawdust, fully expecting the whole hill to fall into the truck...it didn't. But at least nothing broke. I got out, walked to the front of the truck, put my arms on my hips, looked up to God and said, "Now what?" "Take your spade and stick it into the crack up there," He said. I couldn't SEE any crack, so I climbed into the bed of the truck and stood up on the wall of the bed. Sure enough, God was right...there was a hair-line crack that ran the whole width of my truck bed.

After retrieving the spade, I climbed back up on my perch and tried to stab the cutting edge into the crack...it wouldn't go in. No matter how I held the spade nor how hard I gouged, it wouldn't budge. I said, "Now what, God?" "Turn the spade around and put the handle in the crack." I, like Sarah in the Bible, laughed. "Father God, don't be silly. If the skinny edge won't go in, how do You expect a big round handle to go in...but I'll do it just because You said to."

Turning the spade around, I raised the end of the handle up to the crack. When I had just barely touched the crack, something sucked half of the spade handle into the hill-side and it became securely stuck there. After I recovered from the shock of this, I said, "Ok, now what?" He said, "Pull forward on the handle." You guessed it, when I pulled on the handle the overhang landed into my truck bed. God was faithful to His Word...He had moved my mountain.

EPILOGUE

Years ago I wrote a poem about being real. It starts out as follows: "Who am I ..Inside and out...am I real ...or just a rain spout...where are my feelings...all tucked away inside...No! Don't you peek...or I will hide...I use so many roles...I am this or that...always performing...wait till I get my hat...when will I emerge...so all can see...I am a human being...with depths like the sea........" I will now emerge some and show you a little of myself before "Edward" and after "Edward."

To start, I am Lee Ladouceur and I am buying a house in Bardstown , Ky. But this was not always my home place nor my name. In 1932 I was born in the West End of Louisville, Ky., and my birth certificate read Emily Lee Byers. I grew up an only child in a neighborhood where there were only three houses, no children, and TV hadn't been invented yet. I spent most of my time reading books. By the time I got into high school the experts found I read backwards and had a very short memorization span. Today this is called Dyslexia.

In my time era girls were expected to marry young and have lots of children. Since I was having a difficult time in school due to my reading problem I choose to go along with my families expectations. I dropped out of school, married at the age of 16 and my name changed to Emily Lee Harrison. In the years that followed I birthed nine children.

While I was raising my children I continued to read. I had more fun doing my children's school projects then my children did. My father and I would stay up long after my husband and children went to bed looking up extra reading material in the encyclopedias about the subject of my children's homework. In 1972 when I was 40 years old I went to an adult leaning center, took a test and got my GED. In 1975, due to major health problems, I lost everything. My marriage of 26 yr., my children, my home, my income and my standing in the community. I floundered for four years and lived any way I could to survive. At the end of the four years Edward Ladouceur came into my life. In the '70's I had rebelled over the name of Emily and had replaced it with my middle name. With my marriage to Edward I became known as Lee Ladouceur. It was shortly after this marriage that I met the real Jesus.

I had been raised and had raised my children in a religious setting. But when all the problems started crashing in on my life that religious institution had nothing to offer me. When I met Jesus He miraculously healed me and the hidden desires of my heart began to manifest in my life. God had called me into missionary work when I was nine years old but I knew this was impossible in my family. Married to Edward, for the first time I could see how this could be done.

I began to read the Bible with all the gusto that I had read other things. I attended Bible schools whenever one would open-up for me. I studied through the mail. I completed my first Bible School and was ordained in the ministry in the Spring of 1983. Edward and I began traveling the United States and Mexico in a motor home teaching the Bible where ever we found hungry students. He went to be with the Lord that December. In June of the following year, my twin daughter Lois joined me and she and I continued on in the ministry together.

In 1991 I attended a seminary in Fla. and received my Bachelors degree in Theology. In 1992 I attended a Christian Clown School and received my diploma in professional clowning. In 1993 I was given a charter to open my own Inter-Denominational Bible School, which I now run out of my home. These were all desires of my heart, but, the icing on the cake came when I finally reached 65 and I could attend college..."tuition free". Most people would have started college when they were young and then went into marriage and other things. My life is the reverse of that system. But remember, I was the one who started out in this world reading backward. I guess it just spilled over into my everyday life as well.

Just giving me icing was not enough for God. He had candles ready for my cake of life. Today, in 1999, my twin daughter, Lois Dymun, is married to a Southern Baptist Minister/Seminary student in Louisville, Ky.. My other twin daughter, Gwen Cooper, is married to a Baptist Assistant Pastor in Bardstown, Ky. My son, William Harrison, is a Southern Baptist Missionary severing in Nazareth, Israel at the time of this printing. My oldest daughter, Gale Barnes, is a Catholic Eucharist Minister to the shut-ins in Louisville, Ky..

God has never forgotten that as each of my children were born, I offered them to Him and asked that they would grow up to serve Him in the Religious Life.

If someone were to ask me what the moral of my life is, I would have to say, "Handicaps and the problems of life are blessings in disguise if we don't give in to them to the point of giving up on ourselves."

In lieu of a convenient bookstore, you may order additional copies of <u>Miracle Hill,</u> directly from the author. Please, feel free to write or call at:

Son-Kissed Ministries, Inc.
Son Kissed Bible School
406 East Halstead Ave.
Bardstown, KY, 4004
(502) 349-2006

****

In lieu of a convenient bookstore, you may order additional copies of <u>Miracle Hill,</u> directly from the author. Please, feel free to write or call at:

Son-Kissed Ministries, Inc.
Son Kissed Bible School
406 East Halstead Ave.
Bardstown, KY, 4004
(502) 349-2006